Partition Love

Nafeesa Farrukh

WARRU PRESS

First published by Warru Press, 2021

Partition Love is a work of fiction. This novel's story, the town of Firozpur and the characters are fictitious and with the exception of Lord Mountbatten and Clement Attlee, any resemblance to persons living or dead is coincidental. The Partition, however, was very real.

First edition

Paperback: 978-0-6452861-1-3

Hardback: 978-0-6452861-6-8

eBook: 978-0-6452861-5-1

Dear Reader

Dear Reader,

This book is set in India and Pakistan in 1947. Therefore, there are a number of words used in the book that may be unfamiliar to some readers. These words include: items of clothing, such as the chador; dishes of food and also ways of addressing people, such as khala for aunt. These words can be found in a small glossary at the end of the book.

This book is also written in UK / Australian English rather than US English. This means that some US readers may notice words spelled differently to what they are used to. These words include: colour rather than color, neighbour for neighbor, recognise for recognize and towards rather than toward. Although, I cannot guarantee that there are no spelling errors, most of the differences seen will be due to the differences in UK and US spelling and grammar.

I hope you enjoy this book.

Nafeesa Farrukh

Chapter 1

October, 1946:

It was night-time in Firozpur, a small town to the north-west of Patiala, India. Raiqa lay on the bed she was temporarily sharing with her sister, flipping through the pages of a newspaper. She skimmed through an article which she was sure her father would be busy discussing with his friends somewhere. After she was finished, she shifted her attention to her recently married sister who was busy cleaning up the room before starting to pack.

"Aapi?" Raiqa asked. "Hm?"

Najma had come to stay for the first time after her wedding the previous month. Her husband, Hassan was in Agra for a few days for his job. He had stopped by when he dropped her off last week.

"Can I have your green *dupatta*, the one you bought for Alia Aapa's wedding? Amma didn't let me touch it after you were gone. She said that you'd be back for it."

Raiqa gave Najma the loveliest look she could muster, her gaze following her older sister around the room as she picked up various articles of clothing. Najma paused for a second, turning her head to look at Raiqa who fluttered her eyelashes taking advantage of the opportunity. The corners of her lips went up slightly as she turned her head back.

"I'm taking it with me," Najma confirmed, picking up Raiqa's shoes from the floor and placing them neatly in the shoe shelf. "What about the shoes Abba bought you last year on your birthday?" Raiqa asked again, crawling to the edge of the bed. "Those too," Aapi replied without sparing her another glance.

Raiqa could hear the smile in her voice; Najma was having fun teasing her.

"Your gold earrings?"

"I'm taking them."

"Your red dress with the gold lace?"

"Why wouldn't I take that? I only sewed it last month."

"I know!" Raiqa let herself fall backward on the bed and groaned. "But you just got married! You just got so many new clothes, why can't you give some of your old ones to me? Seriously, Aapi, don't you think you are being a little too unkind to me?"

Najma set aside the pile of dirty clothes on a nearby chair and came to sit on the bed next to Raiqa. "I am being unkind?" She asked with a little raise of her eyebrows. Raiqa nodded vigorously. "And you're not?"

Raiqa sat up on the bed. "What did I do?"

"It's my first time coming home after I got married, and all you want to talk about is if you can have my stuff. Shouldn't I be the one upset?"

"Ah."

Raiqa shuffled closer to her sister, suddenly feeling guilty. She took her arm and pulled her closer so she could rest her head on her shoulder. "I missed you, Aapi," she murmured honestly. "I missed you a lot."

It was true. After Najma got married, Raiqa realised how big a part Najma played in the house. She was the one who took care of Daadi, made sure that she ate properly and took her medicines. She was also the one who helped Amma with all the cleaning and cooking. Their *haveli*, although very old, wasn't exactly small. Now all those responsibilities that Najma previously had were solely Raiqa's, she valued her sister's stamina even more.

Not just that, but Najma had been Raiqa's best friend too.

They had spent almost every moment of their childhood together. Whether she was waking her up and braiding her hair into two pigtails before getting ready for school herself every day or making her clothes for her dolls, Najma had done it all. Now that she was gone, she realised that arguing with fourteen-year-old Jamil wasn't as amusing if there was no-one to take her side when Amma scolded them.

Raiqa heard Najma let out a light chuckle as she gently took her arm out of Raiqa's grasp to put it around her shoulder. "You're taking care of yourself, right?"

Raiqa nodded. "I'm taking care of everyone else too so that they love me more than they love you."

Najma laughed. "Go ahead and try," she challenged. "You don't scare me, *bachay*."

Raiqa laughed at how, even though the two sisters were only three years apart, Najma had developed a habit of referring to Raiqa as *bachay* when she was teasing her. It was usually how Daadi referred to them. The single word was filled with fondness and affection when it left their grandmother's lips. But when Najma said it, it was usually because she had once again realised that, although she herself had continued to mature with age, Raiqa's inner child had never grown up.

"The way you choose to disregard my buttering abilities only makes my work easier." Raiqa lifted her chin with self- assurance. Then catching sight of her sister's doubtful look, she burst out laughing.

"Fine, I admit it. I thoroughly lack buttering talents of any sort." Najma patted her shoulder before getting up. "Good that you know. Now go out and make space for everyone to sleep. It's too hot to sleep inside today."

Raiqa groaned. "Jamil hauled a *charpai* to Daadi's room earlier. I'll have to take it back out," she complained, but dragged herself off the bed and put her slippers on. "They're heavy."

Najma didn't reply. She was too busy filling up her small, metal trunk with her clothes and jewellery to bother with Raiqa's complaints about moving the woven, wooden beds. She had to finish packing; she was going back tomorrow.

"Is Hassan Bhai going to come?"

Raiqa paused for a moment, the reality of her sister leaving hitting her once again like it had the night she'd married. Before that, she had been happy with the fact that there was going to be a wedding. However, it seemed to her as if her mind hadn't registered that it would mean her sister was leaving. It was only when she saw Najma dolled up in her red *lehenga* and gold jewellery that it clicked; Najma had a different place to call home.

Najma shook her head, placing her clothes neatly on top of one another in the case. Raiqa briefly caught sight of the green *dupatta* she had been asking her for earlier. She really was taking it back with her.

"He had some work left to do in Agra. He's going to be there a few days. Asghar is visiting us for the weekend, so he'll pick me up on the way."

Asghar, Hassan's younger brother, was around Najma's age, a few years older than Raiqa herself. Although Najma had only studied up until 12th grade, he had continued his studies at Osmania University, after which he had started working in Rawalpindi where Hassan's family lived. Raiqa knew him well. Back when their family lived in Firozpur, Najma, Raiqa and Asghar played together along with the other kids in the neighbourhood. Since Hassan was older, he usually spent time with his own friends.

Their family had relocated to Rawalpindi after Najma's late father-in-law had been promoted to a better job there. After the move, their family only came to visit their grandparents once a year, but after they passed away, those visits became even more scarce.

"Then why can't you stay for a few more days? Asghar doesn't need to come, then."

"He's already coming to visit a friend."

"He has a friend here?" Raiqa's eyebrows knit together in confusion. It was only after she took a moment to remember that she recalled him laughing with one man throughout Najma's wedding ceremony. She hadn't paid that much attention to him, since she assumed that he was from Hassan's side.

"Yes, Suraiyya Khala's son," she told her, referring to their neighbour. "They were both in the same graduating class at their university. He has a job in Delhi now, so he's coming to visit for a bit too."

Raiqa racked her mind, trying to put a face to this nameless man. She did remember Suraiyya Khala mentioning proudly to Amma that her son had a good job, but that was all she remembered. Suraiyya Khala and her husband, Siddiqui Khalu had moved next door about four years ago, and by then, their son had already started studying at Osmania. Back then, Raiqa was only fourteen. Even though he had returned home often to visit his parents, Raiqa had never taken any notice and could not recall him.

Amma and Suraiyya Khala had become very close over the years, they were almost like real sisters. Abba and Siddiqui Khalu were friends too, although their political differences didn't allow them to be as close as their wives were. Siddiqui Khalu was a supporter of the India National Congress while Abba was a strong Muslim League supporter. The violence that had broken out in August was still the main topic of conversation. It seemed that more pockets of violence were constantly being reported. Raiqa and the other women would lament how there could be so much violence and death in their beloved India. She was very thankful that she lived is such a peaceful town.

Suraiyya Khala was kind, loving and soft while her husband was strict and somewhat scary to those who met him the first time. But since their families were close, she had gone over to their house a lot over the past few years. She now knew them well enough to recognise that they were both extremely affectionate people who treated her like their own daughter. It was Siddiqui Khalu who had taught her to play chess, and he gave her the most *eidi*.

As Raiqa made space for everyone to sleep, she subconsciously wondered what their son was like. Suraiyya Khala and her husband had such different personalities. It was hard to imagine which habits their son would have picked from each parent.

"Why am I thinking about it? I probably won't even meet him."

* * *

Najma left the next day. Amma tried to convince Asghar to stay the night and leave the next day, but he had already bought the train tickets before coming. He had only planned to stop by at their house shortly, anyway. He spent half the day at Suraiyya Khala's with his friend, who had arrived the same morning.

The day after Najma left, Raiqa realised, once again, how hard it was to do all the household chores herself. She woke up early, helped Amma cook breakfast, and then swept and mopped the entire *haveli*, including the courtyard where it seemed as if birds had made it their own private eating space. By the time she was done, it was time to prepare for lunch.

Raiqa was sitting outside the kitchen and there was a small basket beside her knees in which she was peeling the ruby red tomatoes. As she did this, Najma arranged fresh spinach leaves as a base for their salad and thinly cut the cucumbers.

"Amma, we don't have enough tomatoes!" Raiqa informed her mother, poking her head out of the kitchen door. Amma, who was busy cutting vegetables outside, looked around in search of Jamil.

"Jamil!" she called out loudly.

"He's playing next door, Rasheeda," Daadi, who was lying down on the *charpai* next to Amma, told her. "The poor kid feels hesitant asking you for permission, so he asked me instead."

Raiqa and Najma joked that Jamil was their grandmother's favourite because he was her only grandson. Daadi always laughed at that, saying that it was because he was her only 'Jamil', just like Raiqa was her only 'Raiqa' and Najma was her only 'Najma'. She liked to say that she had a different place in her heart for all her grandchildren, and none of them was bigger than the other.

"You shouldn't have allowed him, Amma. The kid barely ever stays at home. He will end up failing this year at this rate."

They had a similar conversation every day. Amma worried that since Jamil spent too much time outside, he would end up mixing with the wrong crowd. Jamil was already lazy when it came to schoolwork anyway, so Amma was apprehensive about his future.

Daadi, on the other hand, was very carefree. She believed that not giving oneself too many troubles was the way to live life. She had learnt this from their grandfather, who had a similar personality himself. Although he had passed away when Raiqa was merely a toddler, Daadi loved to tell stories about him. Apparently Daadi had once been the kind who worried easily, like Amma, but it was Daada who had changed her for the better.

"It's okay," Daadi waved her hand dismissively. "It's his age to play. Don't be so harsh on him."

Amma shook her head and sighed. "He does this because he knows you will take his side no matter what."

Daadi only smiled at that. Amma turned to Raiqa. "Go next door and call Jamil."

Raiqa exhaled, picking up her *dupatta* that she had hung on the door while she cooked. Raiqa knew that, as much as she would have preferred, Amma wouldn't let her go out and buy the vegetables herself. The bazaar wasn't that close and Amma was aware that a group of men usually sat outside their houses and chatted; it wouldn't be proper to walk by them.

They lived in a small, close knit community. The houses were in a group behind the bazaar, which was separated by a number of toddy palms, neem trees and mango trees. When Jamil was younger he used to pick mangoes from there, but soon discovered that many had Bengal Velvet Bean climbing over the trunks and branches. He didn't have to do it too often to decide that the resulting itchiness just wasn't worth it. Raiqa loved the bazaar with all the colourful fruits, spices and fabrics. She loved watching people and meeting people she knew there too. Raiqa sighed, it would be better if Jamil went.

Raiqa wrapped her *dupatta* around her and quickly made her way outside. Khala's home was never locked so she easily let herself in and looked around to see if she could find her brother. She knew where Suraiyya usually sat so she made a direct beeline to the door on the left.

"Salam, Suraiyya Khala," she said as she stepped in and saw Suraiyya Khala lying down fanning herself with a handmade can fan.

Her face broke into a wide smile like it always did at the sight of her, and she sat up straight, opening her arms. "Oh, look who it is. It's Raiqa *beti*," she greeted as she embraced her while sitting. "How is my *jan*?"

Raiqa smiled at the loving way Suraiyya called her *jan* – life. Apart from her parents and grandmother, Suraiyya Khala was the only one who called her that.

"Very well, *Alhamdulillah*," she replied, sitting down next to her. "Amma sent me to call Jamil. He's been bothering you a lot these days, hasn't he?"

"Oh no, not at all," Suraiyya waved her hand indifferently. "He's been getting along with my Haidar. In fact, there were a few things that needed fixing around the house. He's been helping him."

Haidar. So that was her son's name. She tried to put a face to the name but failed.

"Ah," Raiqa said, glad that Jamil was being helpful somewhere, even if it wasn't their own house. "We were out of tomatoes, actually. So Amma wanted him to get them."

"Oh okay," Suraiyya nodded understandingly. "They were right here just now…" She looked around. "Haidar *beta*!"

Raiqa looked in the direction Suraiyya was looking in too, oddly interested in finally putting a face to the person she had only heard of as 'Suraiyya Khala's son' for the past four years. She wondered why she had never seen him before. He obviously visited.

Why had our paths never crossed before? At twenty-one he is the same age as Najma.

She heard his footsteps before he came into view, her brother trailing shortly behind him. "Yes,

Amma?"

He was tall, taller than she had imagined him to be. He was dressed neatly in a plain tan *Kuta* but it was obvious that he had been working because of the small beads of sweat lining his forehead. At first glance, she thought, he didn't look like either of his parents. Both of them were of fairly normal height and normal looking. While he was of average build, his arms were muscular as if from physical work. Along with his square jawline, he looked strong, dependable. He was, she concluded, someone who could be called good-looking. Raiqa shook her head, why was she thinking these things.

Before Suraiyya could say anything, Jamil asked, as he looked straight at his sister, "Raiqa Aapa, why are you here?"

Raiqa held herself back from giving him a look. *Aapa* made her seem old, yet Jamil had a strong practice of calling her that, no matter how many times she had told him not to. At this point, she would even be okay with him calling her by her name if not by 'Aapi' or 'Baji,' but her brother wouldn't even bother to try.

She felt Haidar's gaze shift to her. Maybe he hadn't noticed her before. She fixed her gaze on Jamil instead. "Amma is calling you, she needs you to buy a few things."

"But I'm helping Haidar Bhai…"

"It won't take long. You can come back."

Haidar moved his gaze from her to Jamil, who looked visibly unhappy to leave, then turned to look back at her. "I was going out to get a few things anyway… you can let him stay, and I'll get what you need as well."

Raiqa shook her head. "It's okay," she said. "He has been bothering you since morning anyway."

He chuckled and shook his head. "Not at all." He put his hand on Jamil's shoulder. "He's actually been very helpful. There's a lot of little things that need fixing. I don't think I would have been able to fix them all before I left if it wasn't for him."

"Yes," Jamil said, "we just finished fixing a door, Haidar taught me how to hang a door."

Jamil beamed. She, however had her doubts. Jamil, who had never helped around the house without whining for at least half an hour, was voluntarily helping Haidar.

She caught Haidar still looking at her when she turned her gaze back to him. He was smiling like he was aware of what she was thinking. She felt her heart beginning to beat a little faster under his stare.

"You don't believe me?" He raised an eyebrow.

"It's not that." She looked at Jamil again, who was frowning now. "I hope this helpful passion of his remains when we get back home."

He laughed again, showing his white, slightly uneven teeth. "Don't worry." He looked meaningfully at Jamil. "It will."

Raiqa couldn't help but smile at that. "Let's go, Jamil. Amma is waiting."

Jamil nodded, even though he didn't look happy. He turned to Haidar, who waved at him and then back to Raiqa. "Let's go," he said.

Haidar came outside with them. "I'll close the door behind you."

Raiqa wanted to tell him that the door to their house was never closed but didn't. He probably knew that already. He followed them to the door and right before he was about to close it, he smiled at her once more.

"It was nice meeting you, Raiqa."

* * *

Chapter 2

Amma had called all her neighbourhood friends for lunch on Saturday. There was no specific reason, just the realisation that they hadn't all met together in a long time. Raiqa didn't point out the fact that it hadn't been longer than a month. All of Amma's friends actively took part in helping with Najma's wedding, much to Amma's and Raiqa's relief.

Along with Suraiyya Khala, Amma was close with Lubna, who lived three houses away. She was younger than both of them, just a little over forty, and was the mother of three. The eldest, Nadir was a little older than Jamil. The youngest was seven.

Raiqa got along well with Lubna too. She enjoyed their conversations where Lubna complained about her mother- in-law and the family who lived next door or her children. Her grumbles were never too serious though. She was the kind of person who let everything out instead of keeping it inside. Moaning in front of her austere mother-in-law or anyone else wasn't an option, so she moaned to Raiqa and her mother. But her heart was pure; she held no grudges. Gossiping was another of her bad habits, in which, neither Amma nor Raiqa took part, but mutually agreed that it was indeed, amusing.

"They did it again." Lubna was talking about her neighbours now. Lubna had arrived earlier than anyone else to help. "I hope not too many people come, your korma is smelling delicious," Lubna commented. Raiqa smiled as she watched Amma fry the vegetables for the korma. She agreed, but would never say that. The aroma of the garam masala was pleasantly warming. Amma made her own garam masala, which Raiqa preferred over other versions she had tried.

"It's the sheer khurma for dessert, that I'm looking forward to," said Raiqa.

Lubna stopped and turning to Amma, asked, "We're having sheer khuma?"

Raiqa laughed. "You should have seen the amount of raisins, nuts and dates she had Jamil buy from the bazaar yesterday."

Lubna clapped her hands together, making both Raiqa and Amma laugh again.

"Why don't you start making it now, Raiqa?" Amma suggested, before going to the courtyard leaving Lubna and Raiqa in the kitchen.

Raiqa picked up a heavy pan and started heating the ghee. After adding the raisins, nuts and dates, she found the *seviyan*. She smiled, the thin noodles cooked in milk were definitely a special treat.

Lubna soon brought the topic back to her neighbours. "They keep throwing trash into our house."

Both their houses were directly connected, so it wasn't hard to throw anything from one house to the other. For some reason, the neighbours had taken full liberty to throw their litter, especially fruit and vegetable skins into their courtyard.

"Did you go and talk to them?"

"I did," she said, putting a small piece of cucumber that Raiqa had cut for the salad into her mouth. "They said that the children do it. Pfff, like I believe that. That woman has a grudge against me, I am telling you."

Raiqa laughed, thoroughly entertained. There was just something in the way Lubna talked, it made everything funny. "How do you know that?"

"I just do," she said with a shrug. "Asim keeps telling me not to let her get on my nerves, but I'm telling you that's impossible. He says that if she annoys me that much, I shouldn't waste my words talking to her or about her, but the truth is…" She sighed. "He just doesn't get it."

Asim was Lubna's husband. He was a man of a few words, so it was natural for him to tell her that. Sometimes Raiqa wondered if Lubna was the only adult who talked in that house. Both Asim and his mother were of a quiet nature.

Before Raiqa could say anything else, Amma entered the kitchen. "The rotis are all that is left to prepare, right?" she asked.

Raiqa nodded. "I was just about to make them."

Amma shook her head. "You go take a shower. I'll do it." Raiqa nodded, leaving the kitchen to go upstairs to her room.

Since the bathroom wasn't attached to her room, she had to cross the hall to the other side. She took out her pink *shalwar kameez* and then her netted *dupatta.* If there were going to be guests, she decided that it was better if she looked somewhat presentable. She'd always been told that she looked good in baby pink.

Fifteen minutes later, as she left the bathroom, she could hear voices downstairs; the guests had arrived. She looked down from the balcony to the courtyard where she could see that there were a lot of people. There were mostly men outside, so she assumed that the women were inside. She could see Farid Bhai sitting with her father along with a few of his friends. Jamil was with Nadir, chatting away.

The door opened and Suraiyya Khala entered, Haidar closely following behind her. She quickly said her greetings to the men and then went inside. The elders invited Haidar to sit with them.

As Haidar sat down on a woven stool, he caught sight of Raiqa standing up on the balcony. Their eyes met, and for a moment, her mind went blank.

He smiled. Just a small smile.

Raiqa quickly turned back in embarrassed. She wasn't even wearing her dupatta. What kind of a girl looked at a gathering of men like that? She winced at the thought and then hurried back into her room.

She combed through her dripping hair, realising it was going to be a while before it would be dry. Her hair was long and thick; Amma claimed that hers had been like that back when she was her age.

After a few minutes, she got up and covered her head with the dupatta. Her hair was still wet, but she guessed it was fine to cover it for a while. She would take it off once she was with the women.

She descended the stairs that led to the courtyard. She quietly walked to the group of men, adjusting the *dupatta* on her head as she approached. She smiled when they noticed her.

"Oh, Raiqa beti!" Nasir Chacha from next door greeted her. "*Adaab*," she greeted all of them. '

Prem Chacha, Farid Bhai, Nasir Chacha, Daoud Chacha and Ram Chacha were all there; these were all of Abba's closest friends. Apart from Ram Chacha, they all lived on the same street. Raiqa had grown up with all of them; their families were like her own.

"How's my *bacha*?" Nasir Chacha asked with a familiar smile. He was older than Abba and had a kind face. His soft, gentle brown eyes were surrounded by wrinkles, and his greying beard was the same colour as his hair. When Raiqa was younger, he used to pick her up, put her on his shoulders and take her around the neighbourhood. Sometimes, he would buy her *naankhatai*, shortbread biscuits, from the nearby bakery too.

"I am good," she replied, bowing her head so he could stroke it. "How's Alia Aapa?"

Alia was his youngest daughter, around Najma's age. She had married at the start of the year, and Raiqa knew that she and her husband were now expecting their first child.

"She's well too," he answered. "She'll visit soon; you should come see her then."

"I will," Raiqa assured him. "I should go in now. Enjoy the food."

"Of course," Prem Chacha chimed in. "It's going to be delicious. Our Raiqa is a great cook."

She grinned. "That, I am."

"I'm going to enjoy it, *Devutthana Ekadashi* is on Tuesday so I need some food reserves."

Nasir laughed, "It's only one day, we had a whole month of Ramadan in August."

"So, we'll enjoy it together. We're looking forward to it, Raiqa," said Prem.

With a last look at all of them, she turned her back to leave. Out of the corner of her eye, she sensed somebody still looking at her. She turned her head slightly and caught Haidar observing her. He smiled as their gaze met.

It was a little frustrating how he never looked away when her eyes met his. In fact, he would smile. What was more frustrating was the fact that her heart would beat faster for no particular reason when he did that.

Not knowing how to react, she quickly walked inside. As she drew the curtains to Daadi's room, where all the women were sitting, she realised that he was still looking at her.

H*e was a strange man.*
* * *

After everybody had eaten, the women continued to chat in the living room. Daadi went to take a nap. She was getting old; she didn't talk much anymore. The men sat outside, now enjoying their *chai*.

Tired after washing the dishes and making the tea, Raiqa decided to go into her room for a bit before she joined the ladies. She hummed a song she had heard on the radio that morning as she walked up the stairs, skipping two at a time.

Ouch.

Maybe it was because she was too immersed in the song that she didn't notice the man until she bumped into him. Her eyes widened as she felt herself go back, but the man in front of her reacted faster, grabbing her wrist and stopping her from falling backward.

"I'm sorry," the man apologised quickly. "Are you okay?" Now steady, she looked at him.

Haidar.

It wasn't his mistake though. He couldn't have seen her coming; she couldn't have seen him coming since they met at a turn.

"Are you okay?" He asked again, looking genuinely concerned when she didn't reply. Maybe he was worried that she had hit her head on the wall behind her. She hadn't; he had reached out for her wrist before she could.

"I'm okay," she assured him, only now realising that he hadn't let go of her wrist. As if he just realised it too, he hastily let it go.

"I am sorry."

She cleared her throat awkwardly. "Uh…how come you were upstairs?"

"Both the washrooms downstairs were occupied so Jamil said I could use the one up here," he told her.

"Ah."

"What about you? Shouldn't you be downstairs too?"

Raiqa looked up at him. "I just came up to take a little rest." She pointed to her room.

"You must be tired, having cooked and all. It was delicious, by the way."

He looked a little awkward; maybe he was uncomfortable with the small talk. However, he didn't try to leave.

"Thank you," she said, fidgeting with the *dupatta* on her head. "Amma is a better cook, though. For some reason, I can't imitate her dishes even when I do exactly what she does."

He grinned. He seemed glad that she had replied in a proper manner.

Raiqa however was confused. She hadn't meant to answer like that. He was someone she didn't know, a man at that. She shouldn't have been talking to him like one would talk to a friend. Maybe it was the way he talked. He seemed to have a way of making a person feel at ease.

"Jamil mentioned that," he said. It felt as if he was more relaxed now too. "It seems as though he prefers your mother's cooking."

She smiled at that. "He doesn't fail to let me know, every time I cook."

He chuckled. "Well, I enjoyed it a lot."

"Thank you," she said again.

Silence fell between them. Raiqa lowered her head, staring at her feet, not knowing what to say.

"I should head down now," he finally spoke.

She nodded and moved out of the way. He didn't move at first, his eyes still on her.

"Thank you for the hospitality."

And with that, he left, leaving Raiqa with an odd feeling that she couldn't quite understand.

★ ★ ★

Chapter 3

Haidar was a little frustrated with how much work there was to do around the house. Their house hadn't been refurbished that long ago. It had been four years since they moved to Firozpur and since the foundations were shabby then almost the entire building had been rebuilt.

He took care of the work that he could, but there was little he manage on his own. Somebody needed to be called for the rest of the work, the water system particularly.

"Seriously, Amma, why didn't you and Abba get it fixed earlier? It might cost even more now.

He was sitting with his mother as they both had lunch. She had cooked *bhindi gosht*, his favourite. He had never liked the *bhindi* anyone else made, but there was something in the way his mother made it. He loved the flavour of the cardamon and the turmeric. In Amma's version these spices were not overpowered by coriander and chilli.

"Your father had a lot of work of his own to do," Amma told him, placing another roti on his plate. "He is always so busy that I figured it would be better to wait for you."

"Has he been working too hard?" Haidar asked, a little worried. His father worked for the British as a translator, which meant that they had better living conditions than a lot of other people he knew. He had tried to convince his father to quit his job and rest, especially since his health wasn't what it used to be. But those debates had been futile.

"Siddiqui Sahib is nothing if not a workaholic." Amma sighed. "Farid, you know that doctor who lives two houses away, he told him not to work overtime and come home by sunset but... " She shrugged.

"Has he at least been going to Farid Bhai for check-ups?"

"He didn't. But bless Farid, he comes over twice a month to check up on him."

Haidar nodded, relieved. Abba was the kind of person who refused to see any kind of doctor or *hakeem* because he didn't want to admit that he had any health problems. If it wasn't for the fact that they lived in such a neighbourhood where they had all become family, he probably wouldn't have let anyone try to help him. But since Farid Bhai was a close friend of his, he let him do it.

"Don't worry about your father, worry about yourself. Haven't you been eating properly in

Delhi?" Amma looked at him worriedly. "You've lost so much weight."

He smiled. He could gain ten more pounds and he was sure he would still look skinny to his mother.

"I eat just fine, Amma. My landlord sends over breakfast and dinner every day, and I eat lunch at work. I think I've gained weight, actually. I sit on the same chair all day every day."

But his mother still looked sceptical.

"But the landlord's food isn't as good as this. They sent *bhindi gosht* once too…I couldn't eat it all." He scrunched up his nose.

"Is your room comfortable? Shouldn't you get a bigger place?"

"I can't take care of a bigger place, you know that. The one room I have is enough for me. It's not small… it's way bigger than you're imagining it to be."

He wasn't lying. He was sure that when he had mentioned that he was only renting a single room, his mother had this idea of him being stuck in a small box with no windows which wasn't the case. In fact, his room was big enough for another bed if he wanted to put another one in. His own bed was large, and he had had room for a cupboard and a table as well. It was actually quite comfortable for him to live in. It did get a little too hot in the summer, but it was bearable. "What I find hardest to get used to is the amount of traffic passing by and there being so many people. People just don't know each other as they do here. That would still be the case if I had a larger place." But mothers will be mothers, he thought when his mother still appeared apprehensive.

"You should get married soon. Then you can buy a house. Houses should have courtyards and balconies… It's not like we live in a cold country. During the summer, we need to sleep outside."

"I'm not sure I could find somewhere bigger at the moment. As for marriage, we'll see about that. I guess."

"Since we're already on the topic," his mother began, and he knew what was coming next. It wasn't the first time this topic was brought up in one of their conversations. "I am going to start looking for girls for you now. I know you told me not to before because you didn't have a job but…"

"Amma, at least let me settle in Delhi first. It's not really what I expected for an engineering job. I find my job interesting and I'm starting to feel competent now, but I still have much to learn. I haven't been there long, give me time."

His mother had an eerie obsession with the topic of marriage but he guessed that all mothers were like that. His friends often complained about it too. But sometimes he wondered if he had it worse being the only child.

"You'll find it easier to settle there with a wife. And I wouldn't be as worried either. Every time you go back now, I just worry myself sick wondering if you're eating well or not. Every time there's a weather change, I keep fretting you might fall sick.

It was hard enough for me when you were studying but at least back then, you lived with your friends."

"You want me to get married just so I have someone who feeds me and takes care of me when I am sick?" He raised an eyebrow.

"No, I want you to get married so you won't be alone. And don't think I'll let you off easy once you get married. If you don't take care of my *bahu*, I won't let that pass either."

"Why do I feel like once I get married, you'll love her more?"

"You're probably right. I've always wanted a daughter. That's what I'll treat her as."

He smiled. Finished with his food, he set the plates aside and placed his head on her lap. "I am going to be selfish then. I don't want her to take you away from me so let's delay my marriage just a little bit longer."

His mother gently slapped his head, playfully calling him *shareer,* mischievous. But he couldn't help but feel happy. He didn't have anything against getting married. It's just that he had his eyes on someone. He wanted to make sure she reciprocated his feelings before he sent a proposal to her house or even tell his own mother about her.

The first time, he had seen Raiqa properly was at Najma's wedding. Before that, the name Raiqa had only been a faceless stranger who Amma talked about. He wondered if he would have felt the same way if he hadn't caught her at the particular moment that he did. A child had fallen down and scraped his knee. Although she had been busy carrying stuff from one side of the *haveli* to the other, she had stopped to kneel next to the crying child. She had stayed next to him for five whole minutes, talking to him softly until his mother came. He had watched her from the corner of the room. He was captivated by the scene but couldn't fully explain why. Yet, then it was just a thought, but now he'd seen her several times, his feelings had deepened. He found himself thinking about her when she wasn't there, looking for her when he went out and smiling unconsciously when he saw her.

Don't worry, Amma. I'll grant that wish of yours soon.

* * *

After *Asr*, Jamil came over to help. He was a nice kid, a little mischievous, but not at all bad. He guessed that for some reason unknown to him, Jamil had taken a liking into him. Maybe it was because he grew up in a household with two sisters that he liked doing 'boy' stuff with Haidar. "Greetings Jamil, I thought we'd work in the garden today. It's a nice day for gardening." While the houses here were simple, they were much larger than the huts found the other side of the bazaar closer to the river. The houses also had gardens so the neighbours were always sharing different vegetables they had grown. Today, Jamil asked if they could call a few other people from the neighbourhood and have a cricket match. Haidar said yes to his request. Although he had spent his entire childhood playing out on the streets every evening, it had been a while since he had played the game.

Excited, Jamil called a few of his friends, as well as a few elders who were willing to join them for a match. In the end, it was Jamil and Nadim (Farid's son), along with a few other familiar faces from the neighbourhood that gathered at Haidar's house to play.

Maybe they were loud even before the game started because several people came out onto the balconies to watch. Although playing outside was quite common, it had been some time since so many people had gathered like this. It was usually just children who came out at this time of the day.

Jamil and Nadir set up the wicket and brought their own bats. Nasir Chacha claimed himself as the umpire because he wanted to participate but 'his old bones no longer allowed him to run'. Haidar was named captain along with Furqan, Daoud Chacha's younger brother who lived on the corner of the same street. After the toss, they began choosing members. Jamil looked visibly disappointed when Furqan, who had won the toss chose him first because everyone knew him to be the best player.

The teams consisted of five people each; Haidar, Daoud Chacha, Nadim, Ram Chacha's son Prenay whom Jamil had called from the back street and his friend Asim on one team and Furqan Bhai, Jamil, Farid Bhai (who had volunteered to play, much to everyone's surprise), Nasir Chacha's son, Yousef and Haaris Bhai, (who wasn't a resident of the same neighbourhood but owned the vegetable stalls that many of them visited) on the other team. He had just been closing up for the evening when Jamil asked him if he wanted to play.

Haidar's team bowled first, and he soon realised that it was a bad decision. He knew for a fact that his team had good batsmen; he just failed to remember that they were really bad at bowling. Taking advantage of that, Jamil hit one six after another, and stayed on the pitch from beginning to end as three other batsmen came and went.

Haidar's team was left with an enormous target of 150. He could feel his frustration rising. Ever since he was a kid, he had been insanely, almost unhealthily competitive. His friends often laughed at how it seemed that a *jinn* took over his body when he did anything that had a winner and a loser.

As if his competitive side alone wasn't enough, his eyes spotted Raiqa, standing on her balcony, watching the game. She was constantly talking to someone he couldn't see. Someone who was probably sitting behind her as she explained what was going on in the game. He couldn't help but notice that she tended to use a lot of hand gestures when she talked.

He made up his mind; he wasn't going to lose.

He sent Prenay and Asim first; fortunately, both of them did a decent job. After Asim was bowled out in the fourth over, their score was sixty-two. Daoud Chacha went next but ended up only making ten runs before he was bowled out too. Prenay took the score up to hundred and then was run out. In the end, even though Haidar was left on the pitch, Jamil bowled and eliminated Nadim, who was batting. Haidar had lost.

As the other team erupted in celebration, Haidar's eyes found Raiqa. She was there, telling the person behind her how Jamil had bowled out Nadim with wild hand gestures. Even though it was merely a friendly game between neighbours, he couldn't help but feel disappointed.

He wondered if she had noticed him at all. He asked himself which was better, her noticing him and knowing that he lost, or Raiqa not noticing him at all,

Before he could think of anything else, Jamil came up to him with a huge smile. "Next time, you should let me be on your team."

Haidar laughed, "A little unreasonable don't you think?"

* * *

Chapter 4

It was a breezy night, perfect for sleeping outside but for some reason, Raiqa couldn't. Maybe she had eaten too much, she thought before getting up from her *charpai*. Everyone else was asleep so she quietly made her way up the stairs to the housetop. The two houses on either side were built differently. The one on the left, that was Suraiyya Khala's house was partitioned with a small wall, if you could even call a row of bricks two bricks high a wall. The house on the right was Nasir Chacha's, and it had a wall that was relatively higher than Khala's. It was still not tall enough for it to be a big deal to jump over. Back when she was little, she and Jamil used to jump over the walls instead of using the front door. All it took was a few bricks to stand on before taking the leap.

Back when Amma didn't have her leg problem, she used to come up to the roof a lot, especially to hang the laundry. Sometimes, if coincidentally, Amma and Suraiyya did the laundry on the same day, they would chat up there.

Mere bachpan ke saathi
Mujhe bhool na jana
Dekho dekho hanse na
Zamana hanse na zamana
My childhood companion
Don't forget me
Look, so the world doesn't laugh
The world, so the world doesn't laugh

Raiqa hummed the song as she paced from one corner to another. The breeze felt nice as it gently hit her face. She wondered when monsoon season would start.

"It's okay, Amma. I'll sleep upstairs tonight."

Raiqa stopped short at the voice, her head snapping towards the source. At first, all she saw was a silhouette. It took a few seconds for her to see the newcomer's face. It didn't matter, though. She had already recognised his voice.

Haidar was on the other side of the wall, dragging a *charpai* up the stairs. Before she could do anything, he spotted her and their eyes met again. Then, like he always did, he smiled.

Raiqa wondered what she should do. Should she stay or should she leave?

Why should I leave? I am in my own house. It's not like I'm invading his space.

Meanwhile, Haidar had placed the woven bed in the middle of the roof, and laid a pillow on it. Raiqa looked over at the street instead of facing him. She didn't want it to seem like she was staring at him. Although he did have a certain aura, one that felt like just his presence alone demanded attention. She found him strangely interesting, even though he had never done anything to make her think that way.

Is it just his face?

"*Assalam o Alaikum.*" He had now finished setting things up, she guessed.

She turned to him now, since he had spoken to her, "*Walaikum Salam,*" she replied. "You sleep upstairs?"

"Not usually," he said, coming closer to the wall that divided the two houses. "It gets too hot in my room, so I decided it's better to sleep outside. Our courtyard isn't big enough for three of these." He pointed at his bed. "So, I brought mine upstairs." "The weather's nice here." She commented. "The view of the sky is better too."

His gaze followed hers as she looked up at the sky. It was a bright night, hundreds of stars and a full moon.

"It's really pretty," he remarked.

"Is the sky as pretty in Delhi?"

"I really don't even know what it looks like in Delhi. I only live in a single room with a window that faces another building. There is only a small path between the buildings. There's no way to see the night sky before going to bed."

"Then you should enjoy it here as much as you can."

"I should." He looked back at her. "It's hard staying away from here."

"Suraiyya Khala misses you," she told him, remembering the amount of times Suraiyya talked about her son in front of her. "She talks about you a lot."

"I wonder what kind of things she talks about," he laughed. "I hope it's not all negative."

Maybe she was imagining things, but he looked at her differently when he said it. Like he had ulterior motive behind his words.

"Well..." she paused, thinking about how to respond. He was looking at her intently, awaiting a reply. "I don't know. It was just our mothers talking. I never paid that much attention."

That was only half-true. It was true that she had never paid that much attention to when Suraiyya Khala talked about her son but that didn't mean that she didn't remember anything at all. Once in a while, his mother would mention him and share a story about him with her. She remembered her joking and saying that she was glad that her son had inherited only a few of her physical characteristics so it was a relief that he was good looking.

Raiqa glanced at his face again. It was true. It seemed that he had only inherited his father's eyes, which were a light brown and his mother's straight nose. But unlike his physical appearance, his habits resembled theirs, a lot. His laugh reminded her of how Suraiyya Khala laughed. It was infectious, like it was tricking you in to smiling too.

Haidar frowned at her answer. She wondered why he was disappointed.

"My mother talks about you too," he said after a few seconds. "She really adores you."

"Suraiyya Khala is great." She smiled. "I used to come over a lot and my mother feared I was bothering her, but she never seemed to mind. She taught my sister and I how to sew. Of course, I was the bad student, but I had fun."

"Bad student?" He raised an eyebrow.

"Najma Aapa is better at all of that." She elaborated, "She always has been. Abba says that even though I am not that good at domestic work, I'm good with people. I know how to deal with people. Aapa gets nervous talking to others."

"I am glad," he said, "Otherwise you wouldn't be here talking to me like this."

She stayed silent. There was something in his eyes letting her know that he wasn't just saying it as a joke; he meant it.

"I am sorry," he apologised when she didn't say anything. "Did that make you uncomfortable?"

It hadn't. Strangely, she wasn't uncomfortable talking to a man with whom she had only had two small conversations. She was just startled.

"No, it's not that," she assured him. "It's just…"

"It's okay," he interrupted her. "You don't have to explain." She nodded, looking down.

"When are you going back?"

"Is that your way of telling me that you want me gone?" he joked.

She laughed. "No, I was just asking."

"Next week," he replied. "Then I'll only come once a month for a day or two. I took a long leave this time."

"Oh. I will worry so much with you in Delhi."

"I will be alright. I stay between my work and my home. I do not go out or socialise there."

She couldn't understand the sinking feeling in her stomach. Was she disappointed?

"We'll keep seeing each other until then, I guess," she said lamely.

"I guess, yes. It would be better if we could talk too. You know, not just see each other."

She felt heat rising in her cheeks. She hoped that it was dark enough to stop him seeing her flush.

"Why? Would you like that?"

"Because it's nice talking to you."

She couldn't help but smile. Usually, she wouldn't be phased, maybe even annoyed. But right now, with him, she liked it.

He noticed her smile, and she could see that he was glad. His own smile became wider.

"You want me to stand here all night and talk to you, then?" She tried to sound like she was challenging him but even to her own ears, it sounded like she was flirting.

Why would you even say that, Raiqa Kareem?

It was probably the same reason she was still standing there, talking to him. She wanted to blame him, to say it was his fault but it really wasn't. He hadn't asked her to stay.

"I wouldn't mind that. But I understand if you have to go."

"I do."

She didn't, really.

"Then I'll wait until we get the chance to talk like this again."

"Like what?"

"Comfortably."

She felt her own smile getting bigger. Maybe she was enjoying their conversation more than she should. Was she supposed to enjoy it this much?

Besharam, her mind said. Shameless. She dismissed the thought.

"I'll go now."

"Will you come tomorrow?" He reminded her of a child then. The facial expression you couldn't say no to.

"Why?"

"Just because…"

"*Shab Bakhair*." Good night.

How else could she reply to that?

* * *

That night, she lay in her bed, replaying their conversation in her head. It hadn't been long, and she wished she had stayed. Their conversation had felt very natural, oddly… effortless.

Did he find her interesting? She began to question her observations of him. Or did he not think anything of her at all?

She wondered if that was what men who lived in bigger cities were like. If they talked like that to all women. Maybe it was. She had never set foot out of Firozpur, so she wouldn't know. Her insides tightened as she imagined Haidar telling another faceless woman that he would want to talk to her again. She didn't like that thought. Not at all.

Maybe the women in Delhi talked to him easily too. He was handsome, so of course they would want to talk to him.

She shook her head. He didn't seem like that kind of person.

Then what kind of person does he seem like? An inner voice asked.

He seemed kind, like a person who would give money to every beggar on the street. The kind of person who would put himself down to make somebody else feel better. The kind of person who would respect his elders, and would never roll his eyes at them; the kind that would make you laugh. Someone who would listen to your concerns and then try to help you because he was simply just that kind of person.

She almost laughed at the image she had developed of him over the past three days. Nobody was so perfect, yet a part of her believed that he was. Even if he wasn't, he appeared as the kind of person who would try to be.

She thought back to a few days ago, when she didn't even know what he looked like? She hadn't even expected to talk to him and here she was, thinking about him as she was falling asleep.

You never know what can happen, she thought. *You never know when somebody opens the door to your heart and barges in.*

   ★ ★ ★

Chapter 5

The night was beautiful.

Haidar lay on the *charpai*, his head resting on his arm as he stared at the sky above. He had heard about Raiqa from his mother before he came here, but never imagined that he would have felt what he did when he saw her for the first time, at the wedding.

He never believed in love at first sight. He wasn't sure if that was what happened but it was definitely something. Something that kept his thoughts returning to her. He kept sneaking glances at her, and his breath caught when their eyes fixed on one another. Every time they had talked, he hoped the conversation would carry on longer, that she would tell him about herself and ask him questions so he could tell her about himself. He wanted them to get to know each other.

When he had seen her for the first time, at Najma's wedding, he remembered thinking that she was pretty. She was running around the place, busy as a bee on her sister's big day. Every time she rushed through where the men were sitting, she would quickly cover her head with her *dupatta* and would hold it there with her hand as she ran. But even though she was so busy, she would stop to greet every new guest. Back then, he was sure she hadn't noticed him at all. But he noticed her. He had seen her with that child and after his eyes hadn't stopped following her throughout the ceremony. Out of everyone there, she stood out to him. And he wasn't sure why.

Sure, she was pretty. Her dark hair reached down to the middle of her back, but she mostly kept it tied up. She had dark perceptive eyes that looked as if they were staring into your soul. Although she was quite carefree around her family, she would seem intimidating to those meeting her for the first time.

Their first conversation had been rather short, and he knew that he had been trying too hard to appear nice. Maybe she had noticed that too. He had been glad when they had run into each other in her house. Although it was by accident, it gave them another opportunity to talk, and he had held her hand. It made him want to run into her all over again.

He quickly stopped himself from smiling at that. He shouldn't be smiling at the thought of holding her hand. He was a gentleman. He shouldn't be tossing aside his manners and shunning the way he was brought up.

He was aware that he was leaving the next week. He wanted to stay. This was the first time he wanted to stay this badly. He could only hope that they would get a chance to talk again like they did today. He wanted to talk to her. Be around her longer.

Maybe his chance wouldn't have to be so far away.

* * *

Haidar sat down by Suraiyya Khala. "Amma, how did you and Abba get married?"

Amma sat on her usual *charpai* in the courtyard, sewing away. He often wondered where all the clothes she sewed went. Did she give them away as gifts or did she use them herself? He never knew.

His mother hadn't expected this question. Startled, she looked up at him.

"What do you mean, how? Like it always happens."

Like it usually happens. That meant they had barely known each other beforehand and then one day, the elders of their families had suddenly decided that they would make a good match. Then, without asking either of them what they wanted, the two had been told that they were betrothed to each other. And soon after that, they got married.

"So you didn't know Abba before that?"

"I'd seen him around. But that was it. Why are you asking?"

"No reason."

Something about his mother's expression made him feel like she knew something, or at least that there was an ulterior motive behind him asking that particular question.

"Do you finally want to get married?"

He shook his head. It hit him now, that these past few days, when he reacted like that to the topic of marriage, he was being dishonest. Unlike before, when he genuinely didn't want to get married, now he didn't want to get married to just anyone. His feelings for Raiqa had grown. And this was a first. He hadn't even been remotely interested in any female before and suddenly, he was thinking about marrying one.

He often wondered what it was about her. What made her so special that she had charmed him since their first encounter. It took him a while to realise that it wasn't anything in particular, just the feeling he got when he was with her. The fun he had when he teased her, the happiness he felt when she teased him because that meant that she was growing comfortable with him. He liked it when she smiled. The thought of her crying made him upset. He wanted to protect her. To keep her close for a long time. Did these feelings appear this suddenly for everyone?

"I am only twenty-one, Amma," he told her. "I don't need to get married this early."

"Do you have someone in Delhi already?"

He almost laughed at how serious she looked.

"No, Amma, no." He assured her. "I promise I won't marry anyone without telling you."

"You are interested in someone," she insisted. "I trust you, my *bacha*. My son won't make a bad decision."

"Really?" he asked, trying to contain his excitement. "You wouldn't mind if I had someone in mind?"

There wasn't just one reason he hadn't mentioned his interest in Raiqa to his mother. Of course, he wondered if Raiqa had considered him as anything more than her neighbour's son. If she had ever seen him as a man. But he also feared that he might disappoint Amma if he told her that he picked his life partner without talking to her. She had always been so excited at the prospect of picking a daughter-in-law for herself that it made him feel a little guilty. Before, he wouldn't have minded marrying a girl his mother chose for him; he was certain that his mother wouldn't select someone he wouldn't like.

"Do you have someone?"

He paused, not knowing how to tell her about his feelings for Raiqa. What if his confession caused a negative impact on his mother's thoughts about her? He suddenly wished he had an older sister whom he could have told all of this to so she could convey it to his mother in a subtler way. Sometimes, being an only child also meant navigating these situations alone.

He cleared his throat, looking away, which roused his mother's suspicions once again. She put her sewing aside. "There is?" she asked with a smile.

"I just feel like she might…"

"Who is it? Tell me already," she said excitedly.

He felt incredibly uncomfortable but also glad that he had the chance to talk to her.

"It's someone you like very much as well."

"Don't make me answer riddles."

He sighed, deciding to say it. "Raiqa."

His mother paused. He looked up at her expectantly but didn't know what to make of her expression. She didn't look happy or disappointed… She looked… surprised.

"Amma?"

Chapter 6

She hit him on the arm "Ya'Allah, I almost got a heart attack thinking it was some girl in Delhi? But our Raiqa?"

He nodded slowly. His communication with the girls in Delhi had never exceeded four sentences. He would have laughed at his mother's absurd thoughts if they were in one of their usual marriage discussions.

"If she would become my daughter-in-law, I would be the happiest woman in the world. To have a daughter like that..." Her smile widened at the thought.

"But it's just from my side though," he added hastily, making sure to clearly state that Raiqa hadn't indicated she felt the same way. "We've only had a few proper conversations." He decided to leave out the part where they had talked on the rooftop.

"Don't worry about that. What does my son lack? You're the perfect man for any girl and she... well, any man would be lucky to have a wife like her. You two would make a great couple. Like a match made in Heaven. I'll put in a good word for you. Should I take your proposal to her family?"

"No, no, Amma, not yet." He quickly stopped her, not wanting to put Raiqa in that position, yet. "Don't you think you're rushing things. Wait a little bit. Do it when I come next month, okay?"

"Why is that? One shouldn't delay in doing something like this."

"I know but… just trust me on this."

She finally nodded. "Fine, I'll wait. But just remember what I said. Raiqa is a remarkable girl. There are many others who know that already."

He reached for her hand, cupping it between his own and giving it an affectionate squeeze. "That's what you're here for, Amma. To make sure it doesn't go any further than that."

She laughed as he reached forward to hug her. Tightly wrapping his arms around her, he kissed her head.

"My beautiful Amma, my amazing Amma…"

"Okay, okay…don't butter me up. Go back to what you had to do."

"What? I was only expressing my love to my pretty mother." "I know exactly what you were doing. The plumber has been working upstairs for an hour. Go check on him."

"It's going to take him some time, Amma."

"Go check on him anyway. You should be standing next to him while he does his work."

"Fine, my beautiful mother, I'll go."

"Come down for chai by six, okay?"

He was already ascending the stairs. "Okay."

He was happy. It felt like he had successfully passed stage one. But the most important stage was yet to come.

* * *

As the sun began to set, all Raiqa could think about was if Haidar was going to be on the roof again. And if he was, would it be okay for her to go meet him? She wanted to go, and even though he had asked her to, she couldn't help but feel anxious about it.

In the end, she managed to convince herself that it didn't matter if he was there or not. It was her own house, and she didn't need to be concerned about someone else going to their own rooftop while she was on hers.

She had waited patiently for the sky to grow dim, for the moon to start its course. She had prayed her *Isha namaz* unhurriedly, even dragging it out as much as she could. As she was praying, her mother passed by, and she could feel her eyes on her; she probably wondered what had gotten into her daughter for her to pray so seriously. She was usually the kind to rush through her *namaz* and feel guilty afterward.

She sat by Abba as she listened to the radio, trying to pay attention to the news. She would do this often, if not every day. She read the newspaper, she listened to the radio. It was good to keep yourself up to date, she thought, especially when their leaders were fighting for religious freedom, for their country. She had gone to the roof after everybody had fallen asleep, around eleven o'clock. She tiptoed down the courtyard and up the stairs, making sure not to wake anyone up. It was a relief that all the elders in the house were deep sleepers. Usually, it was Najma who would wake up at the slightest sound. He was there.

Haidar stood with his arms folded, looking down at the street. For a moment, she paused, admiring how good he looked, even in the minimal light of a few lanterns. Instinctively, her hand reached up to her head to pat her hair, even though it was covered with her dupatta.

He sensed movement and turned his head casually. when he saw her, his troubled look fell and he broke into an enormous grin.

"I was almost sure you weren't coming," he spoke first, beaming.

"It's not like I came for you," she retorted quickly. "The weather is really nice tonight so I thought I'd…"

"Regardless," he interrupted with a slight roll of his eyes. "I brought some dried fruit."

He walked back to his *charpai* where she saw a couple plates filled with a variety of dried fruits and nuts. He picked up the plate with *kaju* and came towards to her.

"Have some."

She politely took a few.

"You aren't curious as to why I asked you to come up?"

She shrugged. "It seems to me that you're just really bored here. You don't have a single friend here, do you?"

"Okay, first off, I have loads of friends here." He feigned offense. "And second, what kind of person do you think I am to call a lady of an honourable household just to help me pass time? I am sorry, Miss Raiqa Kareem, but I am a gentleman, and this hurt my pride."

She laughed. "If not that, then what?"

He grew silent. Raiqa anticipated what his answer would be, and it was making her nervous. She was curious to know if she was right, and if he would say it.

"Hm?" She prodded further when he didn't reply.

"I feel like there's no way to say this where I don't sound like someone who is the exact contradiction of my previous statement?"

Raiqa held back a smile. "I'm really curious now."
"If you promise not to mind, I'll tell you."

"Shouldn't that be up to me?"

She could tell that he was growing more and more nervous by the second. This was the first time she had seen him like this. Every time they had met before, he had been smooth, like he always knew exactly what to say. But right now, he wouldn't look at her as if he suddenly found the floor much more interesting. Oddly, it made her feel better. It definitely did not look like he had done this before.

He exhaled loudly. "It should be. But I'm going back soon, and I don't want to without letting you know…"

She sighed. "I won't mind. You can tell me."

"I like you. A lot."

Her breath caught. It wasn't like she hadn't expected this, but maybe she wasn't expecting him to say it quite that way. Actually, she hadn't thought about how she would react to his answer when she asked the question. He was looking at her cautiously, awaiting her reaction while simultaneously being scared that he wouldn't get the one he wanted. Raiqa reached down and fiddled with the edge of her *dupatta*.

He watched her. "Is that the *dupatta* I saw Amma sewing last time I was here?"

"Uhmm, yes."

"I didn't mean to put you on the spot. I just… this is how I feel. And I thought I should let you know. You can take time to think it over. You can let me know your answer when I come back next time."

"My answer?" Suddenly, she was confused.

"Hm. I wanted to send my mother to your house. But I want to know your answer first."

Raiqa had never expected this kind of situation. She had grown up in a different environment where a parent would make a decision like this for their child. The woman, or even the man in question, had little to do with who they ended up marrying. They trusted that their parents would make the right decision for them. That was what had happened with Najma, and Raiqa had always assumed that it would be the case for her as well.

"I…"

She didn't know what to say. Haidar was a good man. She was sure of that, not just from listening to his parents, as she knew they were biased but from what Hassan, Najma's husband and Asghar had said. She liked the few conversations she had had with him. He made her smile; he made her laugh. And even then, he acted within proper limits making sure that she didn't feel uncomfortable with him.

"You don't have to answer right now," he told her softly. "We don't know each other that well. I think I fell for you the first time I saw you but that doesn't have to be the case for you."

"I don't really…know anything about you."

"Then get to know me. We can start today, " he answered. "You can ask me anything. I promise I'll answer honestly. I would like to get to know you more too."

"What did you find out about me then?"

"I learnt at the wedding that you had a kind heart. I would have assumed you to be the quiet, *sharmeeli* type, but the first time I saw you after the wedding you had your brother by the ear. And when we bumped into each other at your house that day, I thought that maybe you were like that after all. But I've come to know that you can be quite a talker if you are comfortable with someone else. And that you easily catch on to someone's weakness and use it against them."

She laughed. "You got all of that from the conversation we had yesterday?"

"I confirmed it then. Your brother likes to complain about you a lot too…"

She rolled her eyes. "He doesn't know when to shut his mouth."

"I mean, you do like to pick on your brother who is four years younger than you are."

She paused. "How do you know my age?"

"Jamil…"

Her eyes widened.

"He didn't mention it exactly like that. It was more just part of a rant."

"Now I know why he likes you," she laughed. "You listen to all his complaints, don't you?"

"Not exactly," he said, popping a cashew in his mouth. "I tell him to be nice to you."

"Really?"

He nodded.

"Fine," she dismissed it quickly. "I thought you were going to let *me* ask *you* questions."

"Go ahead."

Silence stretched on as she contemplated on what to ask. There was so much she wanted to know. But if she asked him question after question, it would seem like an interview.

He smiled, like he understood. "I'm twenty-two."

"Oh, I thought you were twenty-one"

"Close, I only turned twenty-two a couple of weeks ago. I work as a civil engineer in Delhi, but my mother probably told you all of that."

"Oddly, you sound like a mother describing her son to some girl's parents. All you need to add is how much you earn and that you own a house."

"I don't, actually. Own a house, I mean. I rent a flat. That's why my mother wants me to marry so I buy a house. She's worried about me living in an apartment all alone."

"I don't blame her, especially with all the violence we constantly hear about."

"I'm safer on my own. Besides getting somewhere larger is not possible right now, there are so many people moving into Delhi. The population is increasing quickly. There seems to be so many people on the streets now, at all hours."

"Do the people keep you awake at night?"

"I am aware of them, but no."

"What about food? You cook?"

"I can't cook anything other than *daal*. The landlord sends up breakfast and dinner. I am sort of close with the man. He's a quiet fellow, but I think he likes me."

"You seem to like Delhi," she observed.

"Well, I don't hate it. Once I settle down there, I would love to have Amma and Abba there with me, but I know they won't move. Amma likes the people here; she says she'd be lonely there."

"It's a small town so everyone knows everyone. Suraiyya Khala likes that. My mother does too. It never feels like you don't belong, you know. It's like, no matter which house you walk into it feels like home."

"I understand how she feels. I don't want to force her into anything."

"My Amma is like that too. I guess they just want to spend the rest of their lives in this neighbourhood."

"What about you?" he asked.

"Me?"

"Hm?"

"I know I would feel sad without all these people. But I don't think I'd mind living in a big city either. I want to see the world outside this small town. But then maybe I would want to come back to them after some time. I don't really know. Maybe if I had studied more, I would have had the chance to travel. But I couldn't go to university."

"Why?" He asked. He looked like he genuinely wanted to know the answer.

"Abba's business was going badly at the time. It wasn't that I didn't want to, or because my parents didn't want me to. I just… couldn't."

"Oh."

She smiled slightly. "What about you? You went to Osmania with Asghar, right?"

He nodded. "We were in the same graduating class. I think we just bonded over how much we regretted choosing Civil Engineering. He got used to it though."

"You didn't?"

"I think business might have been a better option for me. I chose engineering because Abba always talked about how he wanted his son to be an engineer. I didn't even consider other options. It wasn't like he forced me or anything. It was just expected. He chose it for me because he thought it would be a good career, he wanted the best for me."

"But you could still start a business. You can learn how to run one."

He nodded. "Maybe when I am a little older, I will. I can't let all those years I studied go to waste." He laughed. "That, and starting a business requires money. Which I don't have."

They talked like that for a long time. It was almost sunrise when Raiqa went back downstairs, hoping that nobody had noticed that she wasn't in her room. Their conversation had felt so effortless. She kept replaying it in her head again and again until she fell asleep.

* * *

The next day, Suraiyya Khala sent over Haidar with *jalebis* that she had made. He had greeted Raiqa's mother first, giving the covered plate to her. Then, briefly turned in Raiqa's direction and smiled. She smiled back.

Amma went inside with the plate, but asked Haidar to wait.

Raiqa had guessed that she wouldn't let him go empty-handed. Luckily, they had *haleem* for lunch that day. That was probably what Amma was going to give him.

"*Assalam o Alaikum.*" He was next to Raiqa now. "*Walaikum Salam.*" She smiled, looking up at him. "Did you think about it?"

She raised an eyebrow. "About what?"

Then it hit her. He wanted her answer.

He was looking at her with soft, hopeful eyes. She looked down at the floor. She had thought about it. A lot. And no matter, how many times she did, her heart always gave her the same answer.

"I did…think about it," she finally told him. There was silence again, and she could feel his gaze on her as he waited for her to continue. She felt the heat rising up in her cheeks. "And?"

"I don't mind." Her eyes stayed fixed to the floor. "I don't mind, if you…if you send your mother."

He didn't say anything. She finally looked up at him. His eyes were closed, and his lips were beginning to form a smile. He looked as if he was trying to hold back from shouting. His fist went up to his mouth and he held it there, moving back and forth. His excitement wouldn't let him stand still. She grinned at his playful reaction.

Even when Amma came back holding a large bowl with the *haleem*, he looked as if he was having a very hard time holding his glee. He quickly said goodbye and left.

* * *

Raiqa was now expecting Suraiyya Khala to come over to discuss Haidar's proposal soon. However, what she wasn't expecting was for her to show up the next day.

She had seen her walking up to the house from the balcony. At first, she thought it was just a usual visit. But then she looked down at Suraiyya Khala's clothes. She was wearing a saree, she only wore for special occasions. And she was carrying a basket of what looked suspiciously like sweets.

Raiqa quickly rushed into her room. There wasn't anything she could do now. She had to trust that her parents knew that Haidar was a good man. Her heart beat frantically in her chest as she waited. She was nervous, more nervous than she had ever been.

Slowly, she made her way down the stairs. There was no- one outside. She could hear voices coming from Daadi's room. Quietly, she crept up to the door and pressed her ear against it. She couldn't hear a thing.

About ten minutes later, as Raiqa sat on a woven stool outside the door with her restless legs moving up and down constantly, Amma walked out. She noticed Raiqa waiting there and gestured for her to come into the kitchen. She did as she was told.

"Do you know why Suraiyya Baji is here?" Amma asked as she took out some glasses from the cabinet overhead.

Raiqa played innocent. "Not really." She shrugged. "Should I?"

"She asked for your hand in marriage. To Haidar."

"Oh." She didn't meet her mother's eye. "What did you say?"

"Your grandmother loves the idea. I do too. I told her I would talk with your father about it. But I don't think he will have a different opinion."

Raiqa held in a smile, the uncomfortable feeling in her stomach finally subsiding.

Amma didn't ask Raiqa how she felt about Haidar. But Raiqa hadn't expected her to. She was surprised that she had told her before she told her father. Maybe her mother had already guessed that she wasn't against the idea of marrying Haidar from the way she had seen the two reacting to each other.

Raiqa was grateful that Haidar had asked her before he sent his mother. The process of marriage hardly ever involved asking the girl for her permission, yet he had made sure that she approved the proposal beforehand.

That evening, when Abba came home from work, all the adults in the house held a meeting in Daadi's bedroom. It was after this that Raiqa was informed that they were all in favour of the match. She could sense all their eyes on her when they told her as if they were gauging her reaction. So, she did the only thing that made sense to her. Being the good, well-behaved, daughter that she was, she looked down at her lap with utmost *haya* and said, "Whatever you think is best for me, I am happy with it."

She knew by saying that one sentence, she had made her parents very proud.

* * *

Chapter 7

That night, Raiqa was on the roof before Haidar. That worried him. He had sent his mother the day after they spoke about it without informing her. Was she mad at him for that?

"*Assalam o Alaikum,*" he said softly as he cautiously made way towards the wall that separated them.

She didn't respond. There was no reaction at all. Her face remained stoic, revealing nothing.

"Are you angry?" he asked gingerly, deciding it was better to start with that question.

She huffed, unfolding her arms and letting them fall to her side. "I – no. I'm not. But… you should have warned me."

"I thought it would be a nice surprise. You told me that it would be okay if I sent my mother…"

She shook her head. "I was just… I guess I wasn't expecting your mother to come over that fast. But I guess it makes sense… you wanted to be here when she did, and you're going back soon."

He could understand that she would be upset with the timing. She was probably startled by such a quick visit. In his excitement, he had failed to think about that. After Raiqa had given him her approval, he rushed to his mother and told her that she could go and ask Raiqa's parents for her hand, abandoning his plan of waiting until the next time he visited. Like his mother said, 'good deeds shouldn't be delayed'.

"I am sorry. I should have told you."

She sighed again. "It's okay, really."

He scratched the back of his neck, now even more tense. "So… what did your father say?"

"Are you scared he said no?"

"I am on the verge of dying just thinking about it."

It was true. As soon as his mother had returned, he had showered her with questions, to which her only answer was 'they need some time to think about it, of course', which had skyrocketed his anxiety.

Finding humour in the situation, she chuckled.

"Why are you laughing?" he asked.

"I didn't."

"Now you're lying." He pointed his finger at her. "Please tell me, were you playing with my feelings. Do you not like me at all? Will you be happy if your parents say no?"

She looked as if she was barely holding back a laugh. She looked down, playing with the edge of her *dupatta*. "Why do you think they'll say no?"

"Because I live too far away… maybe because my father works for the British… maybe they don't like me… there could be so many reasons!"

He had started a list of his flaws since his mother's return. It turned out that it hadn't been a very good idea.

"So you're not the perfect package Suraiyya Khala was talking about then? Should I mention that in front of my parents?"

"Just tell me what they said!"

"You'll find out soon."

"Soon, when?"

She pretended to think. "Tomorrow?"

★ ★ ★

He impatiently waited till the next afternoon. As soon as they had entered the house, Haidar had rushed towards them. Amma hadn't even taken off her *chador* yet when he asked, "What did they say?"

"Breathe, my boy, breathe." She calmly walked into her room and took off her white, cotton shawl. He followed her closely and waited. Behind him, he heard his father disguise a laugh with a cough.

"Just tell me already!" He was exasperated. *What was it with women and their mysteriousness?*

His mother smiled and stroked his head softly. "They said yes, my *jan*. They said yes."

"They did?" His eyes widened.

"Yes."

"All of them."

She nodded. "Yes! We even had *mithai* after. They sent some home with me for you and your father as well. I told them we would be coming to put the ring on Raiqa soon."

"When? Before I leave, right?"

"Yes, *mera bacha*, my son, yes."

Haidar's and Raiqa's engagement happened the following week. The ceremony was nothing grand; only their two families coming together. Amma put the ring on Raiqa's finger, and Zubeida put one on Haidar's.

Raiqa was beautiful in her orange and green dupatta lined with gold *kenari*. Her jewellery was light, small gold earrings dangling from each ear and glass bangles decorated her arms. She hadn't had a chance to talk to Haidar today, but she passed him a smile as soon as he entered the house. Her smile sent butterflies through his whole body.

The ceremony was the first time he had heard someone say 'Raiqa and Haidar'. Together. Although the one who said it didn't think it was anything special, their names being said together gave him an oddly pleasant feeling. It made him feel as though they were one already.

That day, he was the happiest he had ever been. He was engaged to the woman he loved. There was nothing better that could possibly happen to him.

* * *

"I'll write," Haidar told her the next morning.

They were having their first conversation after their engagement. Somehow, the rings on their fingers made their meeting feel right. Haidar's eyes kept going down to her ring finger as his own thumb stroked the band on his.

"How will you manage to send them?" She asked.

He hadn't thought of that. It was going to be a difficult task. Their parents couldn't find out about it. That kind of conversation, even between fiancés, was considered improper. "I'll figure something out," he assured her. "But you'll need to reply."

"And how will I do that?" She raised an eyebrow.

"I'll figure that out too," he promised.

She laughed. "Okay, then."

"Take care of yourself."

She nodded with a smile. "I will. Have you packed?"

"I did. I didn't bring much with me, so it didn't take me that long." He paused and then laughed.

"What?"

Still laughing at himself. "It's just that I never expected that I would be going back engaged."

She laughed too. "I didn't even know what you looked like a couple of weeks ago. I never expected to talk to you."

He was grinning. "And now you come upstairs every night, and I don't even need to ask you," he teased.

"So, I shouldn't have?"

She pretended to be offended when he teased her. "We wouldn't be standing here like this if you didn't."

"I feel like a *besharam* coming up here," she told him. "A proper, modest maiden wouldn't come up to meet a man like this." She covered her face with her dupatta.

"I want to apologise for that, but then we wouldn't be here," he admitted.

She looked amused. "Amma would be disappointed. Najma would think she raised me wrong. But it's okay."

"You really know how to make someone feel better, don't you?"

She just laughed.

"You'll dress up for me when I come next time, won't you?" He leaned forward, placing his arms on the wall, looking at her expectantly.

"Why would I do that?" she asked trying to appear innocent. She always talked softly and had a gentle tone, but her words were often sarcastic. She really loved to tease him. He would have thought that he would have been the one to make his partner flustered, but strangely, it was the opposite. Somehow, he had fallen for a girl like that.

She watched the look on his face. She realised that he was frowning.

"You're my husband to be, Haidar Sahib. It hasn't happened yet. You should be careful with your demands."

"You don't have any?"

"I do," she confessed. "But unlike you, I'll wait. You should know that I am a *mashriqi*, eastern woman. I don't dress up for men like that."

He gaped at her. "*Wah*, you're going to make me out to be the bad one?"

She laughed. "You should go to sleep now. You have to leave early in the morning."

He sighed. "I don't want to."

"I am going back down." She told him, taking a few steps back.

She knew he was frowning again. Her smile turned soft. "Take care of yourself Shab Bakhair."

He couldn't help but return the smile. "I will."

He watched until her figure completely disappeared down the stairs.

"*Khuda Hafiz.*"

* * *

Chapter 8

December, 1946

It had been a difficult day for Haidar. His workload was heavier than usual. His co-worker, Jhagar Singh, a middle- aged man that sat next to Haidar's table spent his day listening to songs on the radio and doing nothing else.

Haidar didn't try to talk to him much. There was something about him that made him feel uneasy. When Jhagar talked to him, made jokes, or tried to empathise with him, it never felt genuine. Sometimes, he wondered if Jhagar looked down on him because he was Muslim. A lot of the jokes he made seemed to be insensitive in that regard. Although it was highly likely, he decided not to give it any more thought.

That day, as he got off from work, Haidar spotted Gohar, his landlord, outside his office building. Wondering what he was doing there, he raised his hand to get his attention. But he saw Jhagar making his way towards him and he stopped himself.

Did they…know each other?

They were talking now. Soon, he saw them walking away together. He couldn't help but wonder how those two came to know each other and be friends. As far as he could tell, they had vastly different personalities.

Jhagar seemed carefree to the extent that it was annoying. Meanwhile, Gohar had an upright personality and a strong belief system. From where he stood, the two men looked like a very mismatched pair.

Realising that he was heading the same way, Haidar walked behind them, making sure to keep a safe distance so that he didn't accidentally overhear them. Ten minutes later, Jhagar turned onto another street. Gohar kept on going straight.

"Gohar Bhai!" Haidar called to his friend.

Gohar paused and looked back. "You didn't go back home yet?"

Haidar shifted the bag on his shoulder. "I had to work late. I guess I shouldn't have left for the post office during my lunch break."

"You were sending a letter?"

"I was sending *letters*. Plural. One for my family, one for my family to be."

Haidar usually left work on time. He lived quite far from the office and he didn't like the idea of walking the many dirt paths, over stones and pebbles at night when it was difficult to see where he was going.

He sent two letters to Firozpur that day, one to his parents' house, one to his friend's. He couldn't send Raiqa's letter to her house directly; Jamil would get it from their friend's house and then deliver it to her. Raiqa had said in her last letter that they could trust Jamil, at least for now. He was their only hope in communicating over the distance that separated them. It was a good thing that Jamil liked him, otherwise exchanging letters would have been extremely difficult. "You going home?" He asked Gohar.

"Not yet. I have a meeting."

"A meeting?"

"Hm."

Although he didn't say, Haidar guessed it was a political meeting. He wondered if Singh was going to be there as well. Gohar was actively in favour of the Congress. That's why he preferred not to talk to him about politics. He would rather their political differences not create an uncomfortable situation or tear their friendship apart.

Gohar wasn't a big talker anyway. He was older, quiet and reserved. Although Haidar was renting a room in the house next door to his, he never heard his loud booming voice, even when he talked to his brother, Rizwan, who almost always raised his voice. Overhearing Rizwan's part of the conversation is how Haidar had found out that they often argued over their political differences. Rizwan, who was around Haidar's own age, didn't present his opinions quietly; he, unlike Gohar, was pretty brash. Loud enough for Haidar to hear everything through the thick walls.

That night, as Haidar attempted to sleep after the *Isha* prayer, he heard Gohar and his brother arguing again. Gohar Bhai's voice was barely audible but Rizwan was loud enough for the whole neighbourhood to hear. Although Haidar and his father had different opinions, they had never argued like this. At times like these, he felt thankful that unlike most fathers, his wasn't rigid. On the contrary, he was quite easy to communicate with even if he didn't agree with you. With a small smile, Haidar sent his father a quick prayer. He could only hope that, as time went by, and if times became harder, their relationship would remain the same.

Dear Raiqa,

This is the first time I am writing to you, so even I don't know what to write. I am going to ask a friend to give the letter to Jamil but after that, he will have to go to my friend to get it. You'll know when I send one. I'll send Amma one too.

I keep wanting to put every detail of the past few weeks in here, but I am guessing all of that might get a little too boring to read.

As I write this, I can hear my landlord and his brother arguing again. I told you about them, right? Their political differences never let them sit together and have a nice time like you would imagine family would do. I keep hoping that they'll set their differences aside and enjoy each other's company. But that day feels far away. As it is now, it's hard to focus solely on the letter.

A part of me knew this would be the case. That part had also considered writing the letter when I had some free time at work but…that's probably a much worse idea.

*I don't think I told you about my co-worker Jhagar . I don't know a lot about him, but he just comes off as a very strange man. Not in a mysterious way. He **just** feels like the kind of man I shouldn't associate myself with. If I had written this at work, I would have worried about him trying to read it. It's better to do this at home.*

The weather changed suddenly. Suddenly, it's really cold. It's probably going to snow near Firozpur soon. Times like this, I really miss home.

But that's not the only reason. Thanks to you, I miss home more than I usually do. It's a little unhealthy how much I want to see you. Even Delhi feels lonely because you're not here. I don't have as many friends here as I did in Osmania so that makes it even worse. It sometimes feels like I am spending the entire day with myself. I keep thinking about marrying you as soon as possible.

I received a letter from Asghar today. Najma had told him of our engagement. He seemed very surprised; I don't think he saw this coming at all. But he sent his congratulations. He even called you 'bhabi'. Strangely enough, that one word made me very happy. I am telling you this in the hope that it makes you happy as well.

I miss you a lot.

Yours,

Haidar

Dear Haidar,

I hadn't been expecting a letter. Neither was Jamil. He was understandably tempted to open the letter when your friend gave it to him. But thankfully, he didn't. I wouldn't have known how to react if he did. Just the thought that I got a letter made me embarrassed. Thankfully, even though Jamil isn't too keen on protecting me from my mother, he likes you.

I know what Amma will say if she finds out. She likes to tell stories about this girl who she knew when she was younger. Apparently, that girl had ended up eloping with this man twice her age after exchanging a few letters and 'falling in love'. A few months later, she had returned after poisoning him. It's a messed-up story. But that would probably be what my mother would relate the sending of letters to. She'll be baffled by us doing it. To her, sending secret letters like this is only meant for people having affairs.

There was a storm last night, but only for a short while. The weather is still really nice. I love winter.

I sometimes end up going to the rooftop at night. It feels familiar now. Comforting. Even though it's my own home, I never visited the rooftop that much. But now it feels nice. I keep thinking of the conversations we had there. I wouldn't mind us standing up there and having more talks like those. Talking to you was like talking to an old friend. It didn't feel forced. It just felt right.

I can't believe that I just wrote that! I am a little relieved that this is a letter. There are a lot of things I want to say to you, but I am too embarrassed to say them to your face. I've always been the kind to be more reserved when it comes to feelings. I usually just show my affection with a lot of teasing. Sometimes, I end up not saying things I should and then, when someone complains, I feel guilty.

Your mother comes around more often now. It's always good to see her. She made me new clothes and said that they were your favourite colour. I'll wear them when you come to visit. Are you coming next month? I'll be waiting. I am learning how to make Gulab Jaman. I heard you like them a lot.

Raiqa

Dear Raiqa,

I think I have developed an interesting affection towards the word 'marriage'. I swear, never in my life have I been that interested in the word but now my ears perk up every time someone around me mentions it.

I went to a friend's wedding a few nights ago. He's a university friend who was marrying some relative of his in Delhi. I didn't see much of the bride, obviously, but I realised one thing. I am going to be one happy groom. My friend wasn't; he was sulking. Apparently, he didn't have much say in the marriage. His mother had set up everything, and he basically found out about it after everything had been finalised. She's quite a lot younger than him as well.

I've been very lucky in this regard, haven't I?

Have you mastered the art of making gulab jaman yet? My mouth watered when I read that you were learning to make them. When I do come, please make them for me. In fact, make them every time I visit! It's not a demand. Just a humble request.

I'll make this letter short. I am visiting soon. I'll only be there for a weekend so I am not sure we will be able to spend a lot of time together, which is a shame. But even a little time is better than nothing.

I miss you.

Haidar.

Chapter 9

April, 1947

Spring came early that year, or at least that was what it felt like to Raiqa.

It was Friday. As the two sisters prepared lunch in the kitchen, Raiqa caught Najma constantly glancing at her. Najma, now three months pregnant, was cutting vegetables.

"What?" she finally asked when Najma didn't say anything.

"What?" Najma acted innocent.

Raiqa narrowed her eyes once at Aapi and then turned back, choosing not to say anything. Najma went back to cutting her tomatoes.

Five.

Four.

Three.

Two.

One.

Najma glanced again.

"You're doing it again," Raiqa said, pointing the knife at her. "Why do you keep staring at me?"

"How could I not stare? You look so pretty today. *Sundar. Khoobsoorat.*"

Raiqa looked down at herself. Although she planned to, she hadn't dressed up yet. She was wearing the oldest pair of *shalwar kameez* she owned and her mother's slippers. She looked back at her sister with an incredulous look. "I must have been born really pretty for you to say that to me when I look my worst."

Najma laughed. "Your face is glowing; that's what I meant."

"It is? I didn't put anything on it...."

"Haidar's coming today, isn't he?"

Ah.

Raiqa turned away, only now understanding what her sister meant. She hoped her face hadn't turned red.

Haidar was coming.

This was the first time Najma and Haidar were visiting at the same time. Maybe that's why she was a little too excited. It had been a month since she had last seen him. And this was the first time since their engagement that he was staying for a whole week. In the past months when he had visited, they had only been able to have short conversations.

But this time, he was coming back for a week. Still not as long as she would have preferred but it was longer than usual. She thought back to when she had first laid eyes on him. Back when she had no idea what that first meeting would turn into and what the little butterflies in her stomach meant. That was when he was a mere stranger. Now, even though they had to wait so long to see each other, he was the person who understood her. Who understood her even through mere words on paper.

When he walked in that day, Raiqa knew that she wasn't the only one who had put effort to look her best. She had sewn her clothes herself, over the course of the past month. She had taken her time and made sure they were perfect. Her *shalwar* and *kameez* were green, and the dupatta was a dark red. While she was putting on her green bangles, one of them had broken slightly, scratching her wrist. Thankfully, the rest of the bangles hid the small mark.

Haidar looked… better than he ever had. His hair was pushed back, and he wore a simple black *sherwani*. It was nothing special…but he looked striking in it. Maybe it was the smile on his face, or the way he greeted her family, exactly how one would treat their own, that made him look so good today. He bowed his head a little so her parents could put their hands on it, he hugged Jamil like one would hug their own brother and he nodded respectfully to Najma Aapi as he said his *salaam*. Before he sat next to Daadi, he kissed her hand.

Raiqa stayed in the corner, waiting for him to spot her. Every now and then, they caught each other's gaze. She would smile, then he would smile back. Even if they didn't say any words to each other in that moment, the interchange of smiles was enough for now.

As soon as the greetings were done and he sat down next to Abba, their political debate began. It was never an actual debate, since they both shared similar sentiments. They both were in favour of partition and Muslim League supporters so that worked out well for them. Abba had found himself a good friend in his future son-in-law. Their discussions were more enthusiastic that day because Hassan Bhai, another Muslim League supporter, had joined them.

While he was involved in conversation, Haidar didn't even notice Raiqa was standing next to the pillar close by.

* * *

When he finally got up to look, he didn't have to try hard to find her. She was in the kitchen, cleaning crockery that already seemed clean. He stood and watched her rub the same plate aggressively for twenty whole seconds, mumbling something that he didn't quite understand. She had tied her hair back and her dupatta was now spread carelessly on her shoulders.

"I guess somebody wasn't excited to see me at all. I have to say, that upsets me."

She jumped a little, like she was startled. She turned back quickly, her eyes wide open.

"*Assalam o Alaikum*," he greeted, trying to come off smooth. Now that she was looking at him, his heartbeat quickened. And he realised once again how much he had missed her.

Raiqa looked down, like she was embarrassed, simultaneously covering her head with the net dupatta. "*Walaikum Salam.*"

"I had to look for you," he said playfully, coming to stand next to her. "I thought you would be the first person to greet me when I got here…"

"I thought so too. That the first person you would notice would be me," she looked up, directly into his eyes. She was upset, he knew.

You were.

His eyes had found her as soon as he had walked in. In the brief glance that he saw her before greeting the elders, all he could think was how much he missed her. How much he wanted to take her outside to talk with her alone. How beautiful she was. He knew she was wearing green because that was his favourite colour. Her long, beautiful hair was covered with the net dupatta which didn't hide it but instead, made it appear even more beautiful. Her eyes held kohl, enhancing their rich brown colour and her long eyelashes were almost endless.

The entire time he greeted the elders, he could feel her gaze on him. Just the thought, the feeling of her gaze excited him. He found it hard to hold back his smile, to stop the blood from flooding his cheeks, to lift his head and meet her stare.

Once again, he tried to play cool. "I had to greet the elders…"

"All you had to do was look up and smile at me," she said flatly. "That's all I asked."

He smiled now, gently lifting her chin and making her look directly at him. "I'm looking at you now."

She froze for a few seconds. Then, as if breaking from a trance, she blinked and pushed his hand down. "What are you doing?" She looked to the door. "Someone could come in."

He took her hand. "I missed you."

Her hand felt the same, soft and as if it was made to fit his own. He smiled at the ring, his ring... the one that confirmed that she was his.

She tried to pull away her hand. "Stop!" She had turned completely red. "What if someone comes in?"

"Tell me you missed me too."

"What?"

"Tell me you missed me too," he repeated. "Then I'll let go."

"I already told you," she said. "In the letters."

He shook his head. "You haven't told me to my face," he explained playfully, lowering his head so that their eyes were almost level. She glanced around again. He could tell that she was nervous.

"Fine, fine...I'll say it. I missed you." Her words came out a bit harsher than she wanted.

Even so, he felt a pleasant tickling feeling inside. Those three words made him happier than he had been the entire time they had been apart. No written words could match the feeling of those words being said face to face. Satisfaction filled him as he realised that for once he had made her blush.

His grip loosened, and she jerked her head free. He could tell that she was embarrassed, but at the same time happy.

"You should go out now," she told him. "They're waiting for you."

"I don't want to." He sulked. "Go." She chuckled.

"Meet me on the roof tonight, then."

She didn't think before she said, "I'll be there."

* * *

"I was almost sure you weren't coming." Haidar said to her as soon as she arrived.

After everybody went to sleep, she snuck up to the roof. Najma Aapa had been giving her suspicious looks. She was almost sure that Aapa knew she was going to meet him but didn't say anything. She was still wearing the same clothes she had been wearing all day, but she had decided to put on Najma's lipstick before going up. It was darker than the shade she had worn earlier but she guessed that he would like this one too. It was Haidar who had 'requested' her to dress pretty after all.

"I promised," she reminded him. "I don't break promises." "I know," he lowered his head so they could be at eye level, smiling. "That's why I like you so much."

"That's the only reason?"

He straightened himself. "There are a few more too. For one, you're very pretty."

"I am guessing there are not a lot of reasons then. You should be showering me with compliments by this time."

She realised that as time went on, she felt more comfortable teasing him. Now she didn't just laugh when he was being playful, she countered back too. She enjoyed it especially when he got flustered.

He laughed. "Teach me, then. Teach me how to do that. Tell me why you like me."

"Well, for one, you're quite handsome too." She shrugged. "I agree. That's why we make a great match."

"They did." Raiqa thought.

"But that's about it. I can't quite think of any more reasons."

He frowned; he probably hadn't expected that. She laughed. "How's Delhi?"

He leaned back against the wall. "Delhi's fine. I finally got a bicycle last month. After we get married, I'll get a car. I have some money saved, but I don't need one before."

"You really don't need one. A bicycle's fine."

"I want one. Then we can come back to Firozpur in the car. You won't have to use public transport."

"Your workplace is far from your apartment too, right?" "It's not too far, I can manage. Though, I'll look out for something closer."

"That's good."

"It means I'll be home earlier."

"Hm."

"What? You don't like that?"

She laughed at the sight of him frowning again. "How do you want me to react?"

"Don't, then."

"You're quite moody, aren't you, Haidar Sahib?

"You're one to talk," he retorted. "You got upset when I didn't greet you first. And then when I did come to see you, you tried to kick me out."

Raiqa felt herself go red at his mention their previous encounter. Her wrist tingled where he first touched her... she suddenly wanted him to hold her hand again.

Besharam, an inner voice commented. She looked at Haidar and tried to push out those kinds of thoughts that had entered her mind. *Besharam, indeed.*

★ ★ ★

Chapter 10

"This is the last time."

This was the hardest part. Saying goodbye. He was leaving again.

Haidar had stayed for a week, but it didn't feel that long. They had met on the rooftop every night without fail. It seemed to her as if they never ran out of things to talk about.

This rooftop meeting was the last time they would see each other before he had to go. He needed to leave early tomorrow morning for Delhi.

"The next time I come, I'll take you with me. There won't be any more goodbyes after that."

She tried to smile but failed. She could feel her eyes tearing up. The first time he had left hadn't been this hard. Sure, she had been sad but she hadn't been so attached before. She was falling in love with him more and more with every passing day. But he was right. This was the last time they had to say goodbye like this. He wasn't coming back until July, which meant that the next time he had to go, they would be married. They would be going back to Delhi together.

"Take care of yourself, okay?" He was pleading, lowering his head, urging her to look at him.

She nodded, choking up. She didn't say anything; she knew that she would start crying if she did.

"You don't want to say anything to me?"

She did. She wanted to say stay safe, come back quickly, think about me. She wanted to tell him that she would miss him too much. A part of her even wanted to tell him not to go. But she shook her head. She didn't want to cry.

"Really?" His voice was soft, almost like he was talking to a child. "You don't want to say anything?"

She shook her head again, not making eye contact. He smiled. "It's okay." He said. "I'll talk then."

He reached for her hand from the other side of the wall, and she let him take it. His touch was gentle. Like he was picking a precious flower. Like she was a piece of delicate glass that would break with the slightest force.

"I'll take care of myself. I won't catch a cold. You'll see how fast the time passes. I'll be back soon. So soon that you won't even get the chance to miss me properly." He paused for a moment and took a deep breath before starting again. "I'll miss you a lot though. I know for a fact that I'll be thinking about you even before I board the train. You keep yourself busy, okay? Help out with the wedding arrangements; don't let the elders do all the work."

Her own grip on his hand tightened as a tear left her eye. He was answering her, even though she hadn't said a single word. She wondered how that was. How he always knew what she wanted to say even if she didn't say it.

He stroked her knuckles with his thumb. "Miss me, okay?"

She nodded. She knew she would. She missed him every time he wasn't there. Even when she knew he was right next door, she wanted him to be with her. She missed his smile, that gentle voice of his when he tried to convince her of something, his eyes that looked at her like she was the only one in the world who mattered.

"And…" He gently took his hands out of hers and unbuckled the watch he was wearing on his arm. Then he placed it on her wrist.

"What's this?"

"A reminder. I want it to remind you of me." "A reminder?"

"And a promise. I'll be back. And when I'm back, I'll marry you. And take you with me."

She couldn't help but smile. "I never doubted you, you know." "Now you have even less of a reason to," he said.

She looked at the watch. It did look like she was wearing somebody else's. Its large dial looked even bigger on her small wrist, but it felt strangely familiar.

"It's a little heavy," she commented, raising up her wrist a little.

"It represents my emotions then. My heart's heavy too… just thinking about the fact that I'll have to leave you."

It was sad but she laughed at the comparison. It was a bad attempt at a joke, but it made her feel a little better.

"It makes sense," he told her with a straight face.

"It does," she confirmed with an exaggerated nod.

He grinned. "Don't cry, okay?"

"I'll try."

"I'll send letters."

"Do that."

"I'll miss you."

"Do that too."

He chuckled. She knew that he would miss her. There wasn't a single part of her that didn't trust him. He had proven his love with the words that he wrote in his letters, in the sincerity of all his gestures. She wondered if she had been able to do the same for him, to have him realise that she wouldn't give him up for anything. To tell him that she loved him even without saying those words.

"Wear pink on the day I come back. You look great in pink."

She smiled. "I will."

She would do anything for him.

* * *

Raiqa was cleaning up when Jamil came into her room. "I want more money today," he proclaimed.

She had sent him to get Haidar's letter. At this point, they didn't really need to have proper conversations for him to know that a letter had arrived. Sometimes, he would even bring the letter without her having to tell him because he found out that Suraiyya Khala got her letter first. But he would demand to be paid more if he did the job himself without her telling him to. But that hadn't been the case this time.

Suraiyya Khala had come over in the morning and had casually mentioned that she had received a letter. It was then that she had sent Jamil.

"Why? I was the one who told you."

"This is the last one, that's why. I've done my job well." He brought out the envelope from his pocket. "I want more. A whole rupee."

"That doesn't even make sense. Why?"

"Give me the money or you don't get this."

She sighed and opened her drawer, taking out her small jute bag where she hid her coins. "Here." She gave him the money. "What do you use this for anyway? You haven't been doing anything wrong, have you? Are you gambling this away?"

"What kind of person do you think I am?" Jamil countered, offended. "I'm saving up. I want to buy a new bat."

"Okay then." She brought her open hand up. "Hand it to me." "You know Amma will kill me if she finds out, right?" "Which is why she shouldn't know."

"You two are getting married in less than a month. Why do you even need the letter?"

Although Jamil complained about his errand, he had proven himself to be trustworthy. He brought the letters with utmost care and delivered them to Raiqa only after making sure that no one was around. And even though he did like to tease her about them and tell her that Amma would be disappointed, he never once let anything of the sort slip from his mouth in front of their mother.

"Leave."

"I'm leaving."

After he was gone, she carefully opened the letter. This would be the last time they communicated with letters. From now on, whatever they wanted to say to each other, they would say it with the other in front of them.

This was the last time.

* * *

Dear Raiqa,

I started missing Firozpur exactly after I disembarked the train. Can you believe that? I started missing you even sooner. I started missing you the moment you left my sight.

Sometimes, even I can't believe that I write all of this. It's embarrassing to read it afterwards, but I tell myself not to feel like that. It is, after all, how I feel.

I've been looking at houses. I did find a few good ones, but I think I should ask Amma to come visit me for a while. There's a lot that needs to be taken care of in setting up a new home. I don't think one person is enough for all of that. You should feel lucky that so many people are taking care of everything for you there. I can't imagine anyone letting you do anything.

Amma had been insisting that I come back once before the wedding, but I don't think I'll be able to. I won't be able to take another leave like that.

There's only six weeks left anyway. It's not so long. I'll live without you the same way I have until now. With hope. Counting days. It's not going to be very easy, but I'll try to make it.

I miss you,
Haidar

Chapter 11

June 1947

Raiqa was sitting shelling nuts with Daadi when there was a message on the radio that there would be an announcement by Clement Attlee, the prime minister of the United Kingdom, at six o'clock that evening. "Raiqa, did you hear that?" asked Daadi.

Six o'clock found everyone sitting outside Siddiqui Khalu's house. Raiqa looked around.

Ram walked over, "Am I still welcome to join you?" he asked. Siddiqui Khalu looked bewildered, "Of course, we're neighbours aren't we? You are always welcome, mitr."

"Ram, you remain a brother. Our house is your house. You will always be welcome to join us," Zubeida responded.

Silence fell, when Lord Mountbatten, the Viceroy spoke.

A statement will be read to you tonight giving the final decision of His Majesty's Government as to the method by which power will be transferred from

British to Indian hands. But before this happens I want to give a personal message to the people of India, as well as a short account of the discussions which I have held with the leaders of the political parties, and which have led up to the advice I tendered to His Majesty's Government during my recent visit to London.

Since my arrival in India at the end of March I have spent almost every day in consultation with as many of the leaders and representatives of as many communities and interests as possible. I wish to say how grateful I am for all the information and helpful advice that they have given me. Nothing I have seen or heard in the past few weeks has shaken my firm opinion that with a reasonable measure of good will between the communities a unified India would be far the best solution of the problem.

Raiqa looked around. Others seemed to be restless too. "Come on," said Daadi, "get to the point."

For more than a hundred years, 400,000,000 of you have lived together, and this country has been administered as a single entity. This has resulted in unified communications, defense, postal services and currency; an absence of tariffs and Customs Barriers; and the basis for an integrated political economy. My great hope was that communal differences would not destroy this.

My first course, in all my discussions, was therefore to urge the political leaders to accept unreservedly the Cabinet mission plan of May 16, 1946. In my opinion that plan provides the best arrangement that can be devised to meet the interests of all the communities of India. To my great regret it has been impossible to obtain agreement either on the Cabinet mission plan or on any other plan that would preserve the unity of India. But there can be no question of coercing any large areas in which one community has a majority to live against their will under a Government in which another community has a majority—and the only alternative to coercion is partition.

You could hear a pin drop. Everyone's eyes were fixed on the radio.

But when the Muslim League demanded the partition of India, Congress used the same arguments for demanding in that event the partition of certain provinces. To my mind this argument is unassailable. In fact neither side proved willing to leave a substantial area in which their community have a majority under the government of the other. I am, of course, just as much opposed to the partition of provinces as I am to the partition of India herself, and for the same basic reasons. For just as I feel there is an Indian consciousness which should transcend communal differences, so I feel there is a Punjabi and Bengali consciousness which has evoked a loyalty to their province. And so I felt it was essential that the people of India themselves should decide this question of partition.

Zubeida stood up, walked across to Siddiqui, silently shook his hand and sat down next to him. *At least here there is peace*, thought Raiqa.

The procedure for enabling them to decide for themselves whether they want the British to hand over power to one or two governments is set out in the statement which will be read to you. But there are one or two points on which I should like to add a note of explanation.

It was necessary, in order to ascertain the will of the people of the Punjab. Bengal, and part of Assam, to lay down boundaries between the Muslim majority areas and the remaining areas, but I want to make it clear that the ultimate boundaries will be settled by a boundary commission and will almost certainly not be identical with those which have been provisionally adopted.

"I don't want to leave here," stated Suraiyya.

"I don't either," said Daadi and Rasheeda in unison.

"I hope you don't need to," replied Prem.

"Shh, Attlee's on. We need to know what's going on." Silence fell again. This time to listen to Attlee.

I would make an earnest appeal to everyone to give calm and dispassionate consideration to these proposals," Mr. Attlee went on. "It is, of course, easy to criticize them, but weeks of devoted work by the Viceroy have failed to find any alternative that is practicable. They have emerged from the hard facts of the situation in India."

The men looked at each other, in shock. The women looked to the floor. The men stood up, the women following suit. The men shook hands and then each walked back home, in silence.

That night, Raiqa tossed and turned on her bed. Eventually she got up and started writing a letter to Haidar.

Chapter 12

Partition would happen on the 15th August. Raiqa would be married then. But wedding preparations stopped. Raiqa couldn't ask about preparations when so many people were dying, so she kept quiet.

People were getting murdered in the street, and the number of victims increased every day. It seemed as if in most Hindu majority areas, the Hindus were trying to get rid of Muslims completely. Like they hadn't been living together for centuries in the first place.

There was a sense of gloom everywhere. Haidar's father, who hadn't been in favour of partition in the first place was enraged. A big portion of his family would now have to move even though they lived in a Muslim majority area. If they didn't, they would end up being part of the new India.

Raiqa's family would listen to the radio and read the newspapers daily only to find out that more people had been killed. She even heard Abba and Nasir Chacha talking about how three people had already been killed in their hometown. They listened in silent horror as they heard how people treated the unmarried girls and sometimes even those that were married.

Raiqa's heart felt heavy. She had had a bad dream a few days ago which had left her with a sense of foreboding and a pit in her stomach when she woke up. She decided not to tell anyone about it. It felt as if everybody was worried enough as it was.

Sometimes, she stayed on the prayer mat for a long time after she had finished reciting her prayer, just asking God to keep everyone safe. Pakistan would soon come to be, a place where they would be safe and free to continue their religious practices, but suddenly the question changed from 'when' to 'if'.

It wasn't safe to stay; neither was it safe to travel.

"We're going tomorrow," Abba announced one day, out of the blue. "It's not safe anymore, it's better to move as soon as possible."

No one questioned him. They all understood that it had to be done. As much as it would hurt to leave the place that their ancestors had inhabited for centuries, it was now time to leave. Multiple people had been murdered in a nearby neighbourhood a few nights ago. There was no assurance that their own area would be left unscathed.

"Where will we go?" It took Amma a couple of moments to be by herself before she could ask.

"For now, Rawalpindi." Abba sat on the *charpai.* "Just...let's just get to Pakistan first. Don't take a lot with you," Abba said. "It isn't safe."

Abba was quiet. Raiqa didn't say anything, neither did Amma.

Jamil just stood with his back against the wall, staring into nothing. There was sadness in the air. There was fear too, even though they were all trying to hide it. None of them knew what lay ahead. None of them knew that it was hell that awaited them.

* * *

They came that night, not just for them, but for the whole neighbourhood.

It was around one in the morning, though nobody was sleeping. Raiqa had tried to sleep but couldn't. The strange tightness that surrounded her had worsened.

She heard loud screams coming from outside. Her mind went blank as she saw her father reach for the bamboo stick that he had been keeping next to himself for the past few nights. Amma was holding Daadi closely, their eyes wide in fear.

"Go upstairs!" He told the women. "Stay there and don't come down. No matter what, don't come down. Whatever you see."

The noises outside weren't just screams anymore. She could hear the breaking of doors, the cries of neighbours who weren't expecting any sort of an attack. Abba was now ushering Amma and Daadi up the stairs. The staircase was narrow, only one could pass at a time.

Raiqa didn't want to move. She saw the desperate look in her father's eyes and did as she was told. Jamil watched her as she went up and then grabbed a bamboo stick of his own. He suddenly looked older. Like someone who was taking responsibility for his family. Like a grownup protecting the people he loved.

Amma let out a cry, holding up her hand to stop him. Raiqa held Daadi. She could feel herself shaking.

There was a scream, a loud, painful cry. She couldn't tell where it came from. At this point, her heart was beating so fast that she could barely breathe. Beside her, Daadi was breathing heavily and quickly.

Bang!

The door to their house burst open. They were in.

Amma ran up to the edge of the roof before Raiqa could stop her. Amma was sobbing now and Raiqa could see the intruders from above. There were around ten of them, all armed with weapons: spears, swords, sticks.

Raiqa realised that she didn't know any of them. They were people she had never seen before.

She heard one of them say something she couldn't understand, though she could still hear the sneer in his voice. She couldn't see any of them well. Her father hadn't replied but she saw the change in Jamil's expression. There was just enough light to see he was glaring at the man.

"What happened, Kareem Sahib?" This was from yet a different person. He had a long moustache and a broad build. Even from a distance and in the darkness, he looked dangerous. "Where's everybody else?"

Though she did not know the man, she felt that her father did and she could tell that their relationship wasn't friendly. Her own father was scowling at him with a look she had never seen on his face.

"You have a daughter, don't you? Where is she?" He smiled. A despicable look. "Don't tell me. Did you send her to Rawalpindi already?" He shook his head.

It seemed as if Abba had been distrustful of him before. He must have lied and said he sent Raiqa away to Rawalpindi beforehand.

"Thank God, I did. I was hoping my suspicions were wrong... How could you? You're related to one of my dearest friends."

"Dearest friend?" he mocked. "You mean Ram Chacha? The one you were going to leave behind? He would have tried to protect you, I am sure. But you...maybe you never actually considered him a friend."

A new voice cut in before Abba could say anything. "He sent his daughter away early?"

"He may be lying," another one piped in. "Trying to protect her."

Her breath caught in her throat. Amma looked back at her with frightened eyes. She could see the fear in them even though it was dark. There were stories going around about what they did with the young women they kidnapped, after killing their whole families.

"Raiqa," Daadi whispered suddenly. "Save yourself. Jump to the next house."

"What?"

"I don't think they'll go there...there's no one there anymore. They...they killed the ones that lived there. There's no sound coming from there anymore."

The next house. Daadi was gesturing at Nasir Chacha's house. It was only now that Raiqa realised that the bloodcurdling screams coming from the house next door, weren't there anymore. There was only silence now. Daadi was right. They had killed them all.

Nasir Chacha. He couldn't be...

"Raiqa!" Daadi's loud whispering voice brought her back.

Her sense of urgency didn't allow her to grieve for their neighbours. "Jump!"

"But..."

Amma was hurrying back to them. "She's right. Go!" She pushed her to where the roofs were connected. "If they find you, I don't know..." She trailed off, not having the strength to finish. "Don't let them find you."

She was breathing heavily as she instructed Raiqa with a firmness that she never had before. Amma was holding Raiqa's hands tightly with her own sweaty ones. Amma's face had gone white. Pale as a sheet. Her eyes mirrored her desperation.

"But you…"

Raiqa couldn't leave. They were all there; her parents, Daadi, Jamil. Her whole family. How could she be so selfish?

"Do not worry about us," she told her firmly, still pushing her. She was crying as she finally said, "Just go! There's no time. Go!"

Tears were now flowing out of Raiqa's eyes too. Her heart was beating fast and loud in her chest, threatening to burst at any second. She knew what her mother meant when she said to not worry about them. She wasn't expecting any of them to come out alive. But she knew that they wouldn't kill Raiqa… they would do worse. Death would have been a blessing for her.

Raiqa heard the men downstairs. They had begun their attack. She could hear the sound of bamboo sticks cracking as Abba and Jamil attempted to protect themselves…and then. Then there were screams. Loud screams.

"Abba!" Jamil cried.

Time stopped. Raiqa knew what the screams meant. She knew what the pain heard in the single word that her brother had yelled meant.

Amma's eyes quickly snapped towards the edge of the roof and she fell to the ground in grief.

"Amma!"

"Raiqa, go!" It was Daadi. She was holding her wrist tightly and her old wrinkled eyes begged her. "Go. Your father was trying to protect you. Save yourself…that's all you can do for him now."

Raiqa glanced at the wall which she had to climb. It won't be hard. She thought of her father, who had just given up his life to protect her. She could still hear the intruders downstairs. Jamil was down there alone.

She looked back to her grandmother whose hands she still held in hers. Daadi looked at her with tearful eyes as she raised her hands and put them together pleading, "For goodness sake, Raiqa. Leave!"

She held her grandmother's hands in hers and felt another stream of tears leave her eyes. "Please. Go."

Trying to block out everything, every sound that reached her ears, every thought and feeling, she ran to the wall. The pile of bricks was there, like it always was. She quickly stepped on them and leapt to the other side, landing on some leaves.

She hid in a dark corner listening, but she could tell that there was no-one in the house anymore. She was shaking. She couldn't help but think about everyone she knew. Nasir Chacha, who lived in the house she was now hiding in. Suraiyya Khala, who had been unprotected in her house with her sick husband. They wouldn't have made it.

She shook her head. She couldn't think about it.

"I guess he really did send away Raiqa," she heard a voice from her own house. They had come upstairs.

Jamil!

She stuffed her *dupatta* in her mouth to avoid screaming. If they were upstairs, it could only mean that there was no one to hold them downstairs.

It seemed as if everything after that happened in a second. There were two screams, one after another. One, Amma's, the second one, Daadi's.

There was conversation after their screams died out, but she didn't hear any of that. Every inch of Raiqa was trembling, and even though she didn't have a single wound on her, she hurt. It hurt so much that she thought she would die. She would have preferred that. To have died along with them.

She was alone. How could someone like her, who had been laughing with her loved ones just yesterday… how could she suddenly be alone?

* * *

Chapter 13

Haidar put the newspaper aside after reading the front headlines. He had been hearing about the murders from a lot of people around him. Reading it in the newspaper just made it real. He had made up his mind to go back home; he couldn't live with the fear that something might have happened to his family while he was away. He had bought a train ticket for the next morning and had packed all his stuff.

He could only hope that the conditions back home were better than they were in Delhi, where it seemed as if nobody was anybody's friend anymore. He worried about the people he knew here, people who were directly involved with politics. Would they be spared?

He had a bad dream last night, not about anyone in particular, but somebody had died, and he hadn't been able to stop it. Scared by the nightmare, he hadn't been able to sleep all night. From his window, he glanced at the empty street. It was late now, almost everybody in the neighbourhood was asleep. To Haidar's relief, it seemed peaceful like nothing bad would ever happen here. Two silhouettes passed by, walking together. They seemed to be talking but he couldn't be sure. Then he saw it. One of them was hiding a shiny object behind him. He wasn't sure, but it looked dangerously like a dagger.

The two people passed under a light, and that's when he caught sight of their faces.

Gohar.

And Jhagar Singh. The man who had threatened him jokingly only a few days ago. The man who he had come to not trust at all. Not knowing what else to do and hoping that this was only his paranoid thinking, he grabbed a knife from his kitchen and descended the stairs.

Gohar trusted Jhagar Singh, but Haidar didn't. He had seen a weapon; he was sure of it. He followed Gohar just in case he was in danger. He only felt like he was taking a precaution; he never actually meant to fight. He didn't even have anything more than a kitchen knife.

Jhagar Singh led Gohar to a small alley, after which they made a left. They were going indoors, into a small, vacant house. Haidar felt the hairs on his arm rise. He had a certain ominous feeling. A feeling that his friend was in danger.

He had tiptoed behind them, making sure to keep a distance. Singh and Gohar had been inside for about twenty seconds by the time Haidar got to the door. He pressed his ear to the wooden door, his heart beating loudly in his ears.

"Do you have the money?" Jhagar's voice sounded deeper, more intimidating.

"I told you. I'll give it to you in two days."

Jhagar sighed. "You do not understand the work that I am putting into it, do you? Do you know how hard it is to keep them from attacking your house? I am the one keeping you and your family safe. I don't think you're in the position to be delaying my money."

"I am not delaying it; I am arranging it. You know that I don't have that kind of money."

"If you don't have the money, I have no power to stop them from attacking your house. I am telling you, Gohar Ji. I won't lie anymore. You know I am not the good guy here. You're desperate. Then again, so am I."

"What do you mean?"

"I mean that either you hand over the money now, or I will cut off your wife's hand with all that pretty jewellery you bought her. I get my money, whatever it takes."

"N–No." Haidar could hear the desperation in his voice. "Spare her, please. She doesn't have anything anyway."

"Well, even if she doesn't have any money, that doesn't mean she has nothing...How old is she again?"

Even outside the door, Haidar could hear the disgusting subtext to his words.

There was silence. Haidar knew that Gohar was a man of honour, which Jhagar had just attacked. He had felt his own fists ball up; he couldn't imagine what Gohar must be feeling. "Tell you what, Gohar Khan… I've changed my mind. I don't want the money. Just give me the woman, and we'll be good."

"Shut up." Gohar's voice was low. Angry. Haidar barely heard it.

"What was that?"

"Shut your filthy mouth."

"Oh, getting offended now, are we? What if I don't?"

"I'll kill you, you son of a bitch."

"You can try."

There was the loud sound of a punch. Gohar hadn't been able to hold himself back. Haidar gripped his knife tightly and decided to go in. He knew Gohar didn't have a weapon; he didn't stand a chance. Then he heard a cry. Haidar opened the door quickly, bursting through with a loud bang. His eyes found Jhagar Singh first, his eyes filled with a venom that he had never seen before. He almost looked like he had gone insane. Then he saw Gohar, trembling on the ground. The red mark on his shirt was growing bigger and bigger. A pool of blood spread wider and wider around him.

"Gohar Bhai!" Haidar gasped. Gohar's eyes widened and he began to shake his head. It was his only way of telling Haidar to get out.

"Welcome, Haidar Sahib," Jhagar Singh said, opening his mouth, smiling, showing his yellowing teeth. "I thought I saw you following us."

But Haidar couldn't take his eyes off his friend. He forgot about Jhagar for a second and kneeled next to Gohar, whose eyes were tearing up. The pool of his blood was expanding with every second.

"No, no, no! Please, no! What have you done?" Haidar finally looked up at Jhagar , who looked like he was about to laugh.

"Your brother made a mistake and he suffered, that is all. But don't worry about him. You'll follow him soon."

Haidar didn't hear what he said. He was looking at Gohar, who had gone motionless.

He wasn't dead, he couldn't be. He was alive just a few seconds ago. How could a person, a person who was completely fine, a person who talked and yelled and cared so much... how could he suddenly not exist? How could somebody that he was used to seeing every day, one that he had hugged, that he had seen shake with laughter, how could he be just an empty shell?

"You staring at him like that won't bring him back to life," Jhagar smirked.

"Why are you doing this?" Haidar's voice didn't come out as steady as he wanted it. He had only just registered the fact that Jhagar was still a threat. He looked up at the tall man and gulped when he saw him looking directly at him with that hungry look. He looked ready to kill again. Like he needed to kill again. Haidar stumbled back, feeling beads of sweat on his forehead.

Jhagar, with his dagger still in his hand, advanced. "It had to be done. He knew too much."

Haidar wanted to know what Gohar had known, but at that moment, he needed to get out alive. He could feel a disaster coming. He felt that there were going to many more Gohars and many more innocents that would lose their lives. His heart hurt at the thought of losing someone else and his breath caught in his chest.

He had to get out. He had to protect the people he loved. He had to protect Raiqa.

He thought of the kitchen knife that he had slid into his pocket just in case. But he was frozen, unsure of how to reach for it without letting Jhagar know. He wasn't even sure how he could counter his sword with the small knife.

He didn't get a chance to think it through. His mind went blank as Jhagar took one step after another. He subconsciously backed up mirroring Jhagar's movements.

There was nothing else he could do, so he took out the knife and attacked, aiming for his abdomen, the same place he had stabbed Gohar. He missed. Although Jhagar hadn't seen it coming, he had been able to dodge him well enough. But he was startled for a moment. Taking the advantage, Haidar attacked again. This time, he successfully slashed his leg. Jhagar cried out in pain and backed off, but he managed to slash Haidar with his own sword.

Fortunately, it missed his chest and cut into his arm instead. Thankfully, it wasn't deep.

Now he ran.

He could hear Jhagar 's footsteps following him, but his wounded leg didn't allow him to run very fast. Haidar began to run towards the train station. He had to get back home. Now.

* * *

He was bleeding, but it wasn't serious.

What was serious was the fact that Jhagar Singh was still after him. Somewhere, he was still looking for him. He had to get out and get out fast. He had to get to his family.

The train hadn't started moving yet, but he had already sat down. He had time to tear off a bit of his shirt and tie it around his wounded arm. The tourniquet did what he intended it to do, slow down the bleeding.

He knew that people had started migrating from India to new-found Pakistan. He was sure that Raiqa's family would move, all her family were in favour of partition. He thought of what he had heard on the radio. He could only hope that all of them, got there safely. He didn't want to think of anything else except that. All he could do was try to convince himself that they were okay. In this war-like situation, when a friend no longer remained a friend, when it felt like everybody was only thinking of themselves, he hoped that they had made it out alive and to someplace safe. They've probably gone to

Rawalpindi, where Najma lived. He hoped that they were okay too.

His own family, however, was a different matter. He feared that Abba had ordered everyone to stay still. He wouldn't want to leave his own country. He always talked about how he wanted to be buried with his ancestors. Haidar's father's love for his homeland was deeper than anyone's he had ever seen. But he also knew that his father wouldn't risk their life like that. He was uncertain about his family's safety.

The woman sitting in front of him gave him a concerned look. She was staring at the bloodied cloth on his arm. He tried to give her a reassuring smile. She dragged her small metal suitcase from the side and opened it up. He watched her intently as she dug through it. Finally, she brought out a dupatta.

"I don't have anything else," she said in an almost apologetic way. "But take this."

He took it from her hand, knowing that he needed to tie his wound tighter so it would stop bleeding. He untied the small strip of his shirt that was there and replaced it with her dupatta tying it as tightly as he could. Once he was done, she passed him a glass of water. He gratefully took that too draining it all in one go.

She didn't ask him any questions. For the rest of the ride, she would give him something to eat every time her husband would bring her something. He was sitting behind her, along with their two kids.

The whole ride, he prayed. He prayed for everyone to be safe. But even then, his heart felt uncomfortable within him, almost like it already knew that nothing would be okay anymore.

★ ★ ★

Chapter 14

She didn't know how long it had been since she managed to get up and walk down. She hadn't gone back into her own house; she couldn't bring herself to. Instead, she had left through Nasir Chacha's front door. She only looked straight ahead as she walked. She didn't dare look down even when she bumped into somebody's body, lying on the pavement. The street was empty when she finally left the house. From this distance, she could see smoke.

Had they burnt some other neighbourhood?

Her clothes were covered in dust, so was her face because she had wiped away her tears with dirty hands. Her hair was in tangles. It had been rubbed against the wall where she sat and waited, and the clip holding it in place had been lost somewhere on her way.

She didn't know where to go. Everywhere she looked, she saw remnants of a massacre. Blood, smoke, bodies, silence, all of it. The neighbourhood she had grown up in was now a graveyard. She wondered if anyone else had survived. In the distance, she spotted someone. A girl, around her own age. She ran toward her.

The girl noticed her running in her direction and scanned her from head to toe. It was only now that Raiqa noticed her face was scratched and her dupatta was missing. Maybe that's why she was trying to shield her head with her arms.

Raiqa looked down at her own dupatta, which was the biggest one she owned. Almost as big as a *chador*. Without a second thought, she tore it in half, not caring if it tore raggedly or not. She gave one of the pieces to the girl and watched as she gripped tightly to the piece of cloth. Raiqa quickly wrapped one of the pieces around herself.

"Are you going to the camp too?" The girl asked quietly.

Refugee camps.

"I don't know where it is," Raiqa answered honestly. "Do you?"

The girl nodded. "I know which direction. I saw a few people going that way a while back."

Reaching Pakistan with other migrants was the only way she could think to get there. Right now, she didn't care which part of Pakistan she ended up in. She just wanted to make it there so she would know her family's sacrifices hadn't been futile. That one of them had made it there alive.

The two girls walked the rest of the way in silence. They would hide at the sight of soldiers or any men. Or women. Neither of them said a word;

it was like they mutually understood what the other had been through.

It was about half an hour later when they saw a group of about a hundred people. They seemed like villagers loading their stuff into bullock carts. The two girls made their way to them, hoping that they would let them join them. A woman around Amma's age came closer and saw the two of them. Her eyes softened at the sight, and she let them into the mob. Soon, they were moving. Although it felt like she could collapse any moment, Raiqa kept moving. She couldn't stop. She didn't have much of a choice.

The girl she was with noticed she was struggling. She saw the girl say something to the woman who quickly reached into her cloth bag and pulled out an apple. "Have this," she said, taking Raiqa's hand and putting it in it. "We'll stop for water too… you have this first."

Raiqa knew that although her appetite wasn't there, she needed to eat. So, she took a bite. Next to her, the woman gave another apple to the girl. They chewed on the fruit, Raiqa's companion turned to her. "I am Rani," she said.

"Raiqa," she replied.

"Thank you." She was still holding the dupatta that Raiqa had given her.

"Did everyone die in your family too?" Raiqa asked bluntly. It was only after that she wondered why she said it.

The girl didn't seem to mind. "I don't have a family. I lived with the family I worked for. They ran away before. So, when they…when they attacked, they took me with them." She snorted. "I knew one of them. He used to stand on the street and say weird things when I passed. He was probably the one who told them that I was left behind, so they could take me.

"Took you?"

A small bitter smile appeared on her face. "I ran away. But I saw them with the others…" She gulped. "They…"

She didn't finish but Raiqa knew what she was going to say. That was what Amma was afraid of, what Daadi was afraid of. Before now, she hadn't given a thought to all those who had been taken. Now she looked at Rani and shuddered at the thought of what Rani had seen.

They didn't talk much for the rest of the way. It was almost night again. They had walked about half a day and had only stopped once, and only for about an hour. Raiqa understood; the more they stopped, the more they were at risk.

Then she saw a group of people standing ahead of them. People who weren't a part of them. People who seemed like they were waiting for them.

* * *

Everywhere Raiqa looked, there was only chaos. Raiqa felt numb. She felt guilty she wasn't crying, terrified she wouldn't make it and felt so overwhelmed she thought she would crumble to the ground any minute. Yet, she didn't but kept placing one foot in front of another. Women were begging for their children to be spared, men were offering all they had in their bags, cash, jewellery, anything to let them cross over to Pakistan. The two countries hadn't even been made official yet.

Raiqa had run to hide behind a small hill of sand. Even though there was no one on this side right now, it wouldn't take long for them to find her. Rani was no longer with her, and neither was the woman that had given her the apple. It was utter chaos. And she had no idea how to escape.

"No, no please no. Spare my wife please!" She heard a man cry out. "She's carrying my child. Please."

She saw the woman he was hiding behind himself. She was obviously pregnant.

Raiqa closed her eyes as the man in front of them, who clearly didn't care, speared the man and then his wife without hesitation. She slowly opened her eyes, only to see him stabbing the woman in the belly once again for a good measure.

"Ya'Allah, save us. Please save us." The prayer stayed on her lips for a long time. "Save us, please!"

She looked around in search of a shelter, of any place where she could go but it was of no use. They were on a plain, and there were no houses around.

"Ya'Allah, please help."

With every passing second, she could see more bodies falling, more people getting closer to where she was hiding.

"My God will never forgive you," a woman yelled. "You will see your mother, your sister, your whole family die the same way you killed mine. You can kill me, but this is my *baddua* to you. I curse you all! You will never see happiness in your life. You'll never be able to sleep well at night."

The man in front of her laughed loudly. "Bibi, worry about yourself right now."

And he speared her right through her chest. "Ya'Allah, please let this stop!"

She had curled herself into a ball trying to shrink as much as possible.

"Put your weapons down!" Someone yelled over the commotion.

It seemed her prayer had been answered. She heard a gun fire. A group of soldiers were advancing towards them, and she hoped that they were here to help.

It seemed as though they were. The guns in their hands had scared their attackers, since the majority of their weapons were daggers, bamboo sticks, swords and spears. The group of soldiers had about the same amount of people, only they were better armed. She watched as the muggers backed off at the command of the one who was in charge. They placed their weapons down on the ground, and soon they were running away.

The one in charge of the soldiers was a middle-aged man with a tilaka on his forehead. He didn't say much, only requested the ones who were left to come together and promised to help them to Pakistan safely.

There weren't many of them left, but they did as they were told. Raiqa searched for Rani, and found her next to a body. As she looked at the body, she recognised the woman who had been with them. The one who had allowed them to accompany them, the one who had fed them. The woman who she yet had to thank.

She saw Rani wipe off a tear and stand up. "Thank you, Khala."

"*Inna Lillahi Wa Inna Ilaihi Rajioon.*" The last prayer for their rescuer left Raiqa's lips.

They were walking together, neither of them said a single word.

And they wouldn't until they reached their destination.

★ ★ ★

Chapter 15

Haidar stood outside his house, hoping that he wouldn't find anyone there. The building looked the same as it always had, like nothing had happened in that place at all. Like any moment, he would hear the voices of his family coming from inside.

But when he looked around, he could tell that everything had changed.

In the distance, he could hear soldiers. There was nobody else there, just them. Not wanting to be seen, he quickly entered the open doors of his house. Though he didn't dare open his eyes.

They've left already, he told himself. *They are safe.*

He opened his eyes, letting out a sigh of relief when all he saw was a familiar courtyard. The pot plants still lining each wall. Abba's usual sitting space. His radio. But then…

The blood. A trail of blood.

He stopped breathing. His body went cold. "It can't be! Please no!"

He forced his legs to move but they felt heavy, and it was hard to take even a single step. He suddenly felt dizzy.

He saw her *dupatta* first, on the ground, soaked in blood. His eyes searched the place hastily for his mother, his heart hoping that he wouldn't see anything.

"Amma!"

He saw her.

She was there on the ground, bloody from head to toe. And right next to her was his father. They were holding on to each other. They had been trying to protect one another till their last breath. But the one who hunted them did not care.

"Abba?"

He barely heard himself. He couldn't move forward; he couldn't even blink. His eyes fixed on his parents, the ones who he had seen happy and alive. Gone. They were no longer there. And he was.

Instead of walking towards them, he felt himself back away. His body moved of its own accord, taking one step backwards after another. He felt disoriented. His mind refused to believe what his eyes saw. It couldn't be. They couldn't be dead. It wasn't possible.

He didn't know when it was that he left the house but suddenly he was out on the street. Even though the sun was shining, his body felt cold. His legs felt wobbly, like they would give out at any second.

He heard a woman let out a loud cry behind him. He turned around. Lubna Aapa was on her knees.

He rushed towards and supported her with his arms, worried that she might lose consciousness. But that's not what it was. She hadn't collapsed because she was sick. Haidar wondered where her husband was, a feeling of dread ran through his body.

"Farid!" she cried out her husband's name. "Farid!"

"Lubna Aapa? Where is he?" he asked, still supporting her with his arms. "Where is Farid Bhai?"

She paused and looked at him through empty eyes. "He's dead," she said suddenly, her face no longer showing any emotion. "That son of a bitch left me. He followed his mother there too!" She pointed at the sky bitterly.

Haidar closed his eyes and took a deep breath. He didn't know what to say. He had just found his own family dead. He wasn't sure what position he was in.

"Aapa," he began, then hesitated. He had nothing to say.

But Aapa did. "Your father didn't want to move. Your mother was afraid when I saw her last. I heard that they attacked your house before they attacked ours... they attacked the whole neighbourhood. Some survived, most didn't. Some... some girls... they took some girls..."

Haidar's breath caught.

"What about Kareem Sahib and his family?" he asked slowly.

"All killed. From what I heard, they couldn't find Raiqa. Maybe Kareem Sahib sent her beforehand. But the rest of them…"

Haidar's hand fell off Aapa's shoulder. He suddenly had no strength in his body anymore. All at once, he felt alone. They were all dead. All his people. The ones who had become family. All gone. After his engagement, he had found another place to call home.

Raiqa's parents treated him like their own child. Her mother who cooked his favourite dishes every time he visited, the one who made him eat and eat until he would feel too full to have anything the rest of the day. That was how she expressed her love for him. Raiqa's father, Kareem Chacha, who would make him sit down to discuss serious matters like one did with their real son. Jamil, the young kid who had his whole life ahead of him. The kid who would complain about his sister but would also do anything for her. His eyes had been full of wonder, and Haidar had always thought that he would grow up to be a great man. But he hadn't had the chance.

Lubna Aapa stared at him. "Even if she made it out of here, it's hard to know if she will make it to Pakistan or not."

Haidar stared at the ground of the dusty alley he had lived in. Only this time, it was red. The place where he had made so many good memories in the past four years was now the place that would haunt his nightmares.

There was another scream, a blood curdling scream.

Haidar's head snapped in the direction of the sound, only to see three armed men coming toward them. Quickly, he pulled Lubna Aapa's arm and guided her to a small alley to the right. He attempted to run but Aapa stopped moving, her eyes glued to the advancing men.

"They saw me," she whispered. Just then, Haidar heard a laugh.

"There's another one."

"You go," Lubna said hastily, pushing him. "You still have hope that your Raiqa may still be alive…I have nothing else to live for. If anything, I might end up killing myself. Please," she held both her hands in front of him. Let me die a hero and not a coward."

Haidar could hear the footsteps getting closer. Their voices were getting louder. "It's Farid's woman, isn't it?"

"Go!" Lubna reached for the door to a house on her right and pushed him inside before he had a chance to react. For a woman so small, she seemed to have a lot of strength. She shoved him through the door so he could hide.

Haidar stood there, frozen, his heart pounding fiercely in his chest.

The footsteps stopped, and he knew they were there. Right outside.

"You were the lucky one in your family. You lived." Haidar could hear the ridicule in his voice, whoever he was. Lubna said nothing. Maybe she wanted to get it over with, as soon as possible.

"You have nothing to say?"

"You killed my husband, my kids, my mother-in-law, my friends." Her voice, although weak, was full of spite. "I have a lot to say."

"Then say it."

"My husband, the one you killed, he always told me not to waste my words on useless people."

"Oh really? Then what did he think you should do with them?"

"Sadly, I never asked him that."

"That's a shame. What do you think should be done with people like us then?"

She spat in his face.

Haidar couldn't have said he was sure, but with the cursing that accompanied it, it couldn't have been anything else.

After that, everything happened quickly. Maybe that's how Aapa wanted it. Haidar heard one of them bring out his sword and then *slash*. Aapa didn't scream at first, there was only the sound of a sharp intake of breath. A few seconds later, she screamed. Then he heard her body slump to the ground.

Haidar was frozen. He didn't move, at all. Haidar heard them leave, casually starting up a conversation as if the dead person behind them wasn't there at all. He waited for some time; he couldn't tell how long. Maybe fifteen minutes, maybe half an hour. He sat on the cold floor of an unfamiliar house, a house that had been filled with life once.

By the time, he came out, Lubna Aapa had turned white. She was lying in a dark red pool of her own blood. Haidar only now realised why she had screamed. She was bleeding from the front and back. They had slashed her at the back first. Then they had stabbed her. Right in her chest.

Haidar held back a sob and heard himself whimper like a child. He had let someone die for him. Just like that. That wasn't why he had come back to Firozpur. He had come to protect his own family. Instead, he had let someone else die, again.

He couldn't think of what to do. He stared at her body. He wanted to bury Aapa properly, somewhere where her body could be safe. He couldn't. He knew he couldn't take her anywhere. There wasn't anywhere safe.

You still have hope that your Raiqa may be alive. Let me die a hero and not a coward. You weren't the coward, Aapa. Haidar stepped back slowly, feeling a tear come down his cheek. *I was.*

And then, exactly like a coward, he ran.

★ ★ ★

Chapter 16

That night, Haidar boarded a train for Rawalpindi.

He saw the family in front him, a big one who had managed to make it here together. There were seven of them, a man, a woman and their five kids. The eldest was about fifteen while the youngest didn't look older than five. The mother constantly counted them, as If she was scared that she would lose one of them in the crowded train.

There were more people on the train than he imagined. People were fleeing and all anyone cared about was getting a spot on the train. The floor, the top, or just hanging by the door, not many cared anymore.

Haidar had seated himself on a proper seat, but gave it up when he saw a number of elders and women on the train. His seat was now occupied by a pregnant woman. Her husband stood extremely close.

The train suddenly came to an abrupt halt, and everybody was pushed forward. He saw fear taking over everybody's faces, and he was sure his face mirrored theirs. He heard howls before he heard screams. He thought of the trains that had reached their destinations with not a single survivor because they were attacked by mobs. The blood trains. News of them had constantly reached him in Delhi.

He carefully looked out the window and spotted a few men entering the carriage in front of theirs. They would be here any second. The pregnant woman was holding her husband's hand, who was trying to hide her behind himself. The parents of the kids were attempting to do the same.

There were more wails from the front carriage. He heard cries of men and women, begging for their families to be spared.

And then they came in.

Multiple men, just running through the carriage, almost like maniacs, attacking whomever was in their way.

He looked back and saw a man jump off the train. Deciding to do exactly that, he pushed himself backward as well. Soon, a few others were doing the same.

He felt a sharp pain in his ankle as he twisted it when he landed but knew that he needed to hide. So, he got up and ran as fast as he could, not knowing where he was heading. There was blood coming from his head. He had hit it on a rock when he fell. He could feel the blood stream down over the side of his face.

His vision was blurring, and he could feel strength draining from his legs.

I need to find somewhere safe.

That was his last thought before he hit the ground.

* * *

"Who is he?"

"I don't know. He's bleeding. I think he was with the migrants who were attacked."

He heard their voices but had no strength to open his eyes. There was a sharp pain in his arm and leg, and his head was throbbing. *Who did these unknown voices belong to? Had he been in a fight?* And then he remembered. The screams, swords, spears, pain-filled cries, the sick laughs. He remembered everything now. The voices around him suddenly became quiet.

"Putr?" It was a woman's voice with a Punjabi accent. She was calling him son.

His own mother's face flashed before his closed lids. He remembered her dead body just lying there. *Amma!*

A hand gently held his own. "Putr, wake up. Come on, my son."

"*Amma.*"

Nobody said anything.

He tried opening his eyes and suddenly realised that he had been crying. He didn't think it was because of the physical pain.

The woman noticed him trying to open his eyes.

"Get water, Panaya." The woman told someone. He heard footsteps leaving.

His eyes opened a little, and he was momentarily blinded by the bright light. It took a while for him to get used to it. He was in a small room. The ceiling was straw and the walls were mud. He had ended up in a nearby village.

The woman sitting with him was in her late fifties. She was small-framed and had kind eyes. The man next to her was in his thirties and wore an orange turban.

"Were you going to Pakistan?" She asked.

He stayed quiet. He wasn't sure if he could trust anyone yet.

She tried again. "Are you hungry?"

A young girl, about ten years old entered the room with a steel glass. She handed it to the woman, who handed it to him.

"You don't have to talk, son. Here, drink some water." He drank quickly.

* * *

He soon found out that the man's name was Palvindar, and he was a farmer. There were four people living in the house. The older woman was his mother, and they all called her Ma Ji. Palvindar had two children, Panaya and little Yuvraj.

Ma Ji asked Palvindar to take care of Haidar's wounds and then give him a fresh set of clothes. Now that he had been awake for a few hours, Haidar's injuries began to hurt more. The wound on his head wasn't serious enough to require stitches, but his arm injury was. It had worsened, so Palvindar had called a doctor from a nearby clinic. He cleaned his wounds and had closed the cut with stitches. The rest of his injuries consisted of scratches on various spots of his body.

Palvindar looked at him worriedly as he handed him the change of clothes. "Stay here for a while, brother. I understand why you would want to go, but it's safer here. We'll keep you safe."

He thought of all the people he had seen back home. People who dressed the same as the man in front of him, the ones who even talked like him. He realised that he was scared of him. He didn't know who to trust, and he was afraid that anybody could be an enemy.

Palvindar read his face. He smiled softly. "I can understand what you must be feeling. Even in this small village, I've seen people who have known each other for years turn into enemies. If you don't trust us, we understand. I don't know how to convince you to trust us."

He remained silent.

"Go change into these," Palvindar pointed at the clothes. "Give your dirty ones to me. I'll throw them away."

There was no use in keeping them. They were torn and covered in blood.

"Thank you," Haidar muttered before entering their small bathroom.

"Call me if you can't put on the shirt. Don't try too hard to do it yourself. You'll rip out your stitches."

Without looking back, he nodded. He put on the shalwar first. Even though it hurt, he still managed to do it. But putting on the kameez was harder. It hurt when he lifted his arm.

"Bhaiya?" he called quietly. Thankfully, almost as if he was expecting it, Palvindar appeared.

After he had helped him into the shirt, he guided him into another small room. Haidar realised that their house wasn't that big. It only had three rooms, a single bathroom and a small courtyard. He heard some animals outside.

"You can stay here," Palvindar told him.

There was only a single *charpai* in the room and a small mirror. He wondered whose room it was that his host was offering him. "Thank you," he said again. He didn't know what else to say.

He had questions. Why were they helping him? Why did they bring him here when they knew it was dangerous to give shelter to a Muslim?

"Call me if you need anything. Don't hesitate. You just called me 'brother'. Even if you're only here for a little while, think of me as your brother." With that, he left Haidar alone, with thoughts he didn't want to think.

* * *

The next morning, he hesitated to leave his room. But it turned out that he didn't have to. Around nine, his host came in with breakfast, a roti and chai.

He took it and quietly sat on the bed, not expecting his host to do the same. But he did.

They ate in silence at first. It was five minutes later that Palvindar spoke.

"My wife was in Pakistan," he began, making Haidar look up. "She didn't make it. The train that reached Jalalabad full of dead bodies, she was on it."

Haidar opened his mouth to speak but he cut him off.

"I am not doing this for you. There's this guilt... I wasn't able to protect her. I guess I am doing this to make myself feel better. I am going to send you back to Pakistan. Safe."

Haidar wondered if people like this existed. Instead of wanting to take revenge for his wife, he was going to help another person reach Pakistan.

"I'm not going to ask you to trust me." He was still talking. "I am not sure if I completely trust you either. I'm just asking you to let me do this. I beg you."

He picked up the empty plates and prepared to leave. Haidar didn't miss the single tear that left his eyes before he turned away.

"Palvindar Bhaiya," he called just as he was about to leave. He turned around. "My name is Haidar."

* * *

"Putr, here you go. Eat your breakfast."

Ma Ji entered his room with food. He quickly stood up, took the plates from her and took her hand to guide her in.

"Sukriya, Ma Ji," he thanked her.

"Our food isn't exactly..." She sat down next to him.

"It's okay." He stopped her midway. It was true that he had grown up in better conditions than this, but his mother had taught him to remain humble.

"You're a good kid." The old woman patted his head with her bony hand. "Your parents raised you well."

She was weak. A short woman who looked much older than she was, with wrinkles all over her skin, but her eyes were kind. They reminded him of Raiqa's grandmother's eyes that always looked at him so fondly. He smiled sadly at that. "My Amma would be glad to know you said that."

"I am sure she's in a better place now."

She had to be.

Ma Ji left soon after that, leaving him with thoughts about his family again. They had died innocent. But they had died. And he was still here. Alone.

Everyone else in the house treated him well too. Ma Ji would make him breakfast and dinner, and although they didn't have many resources, they made sure that he was comfortable.

In return, Haidar tried to make sure that he wasn't inconveniencing them. Other than helping with the farm, Haidar would help Ma Ji clean up the house and assist the kids with their studies. Palvindar himself had never been to school but he wanted his children to go. During one of their conversations, Haidar had found out that the other villagers had tried to talk Palvindar into making Yuvraj help him on the farm instead. They had believed that sending them, especially Panaya, was a waste of time and money. But Palvindar had persisted.

Haidar didn't know how long his stay there was going to be. But he wanted to make sure that the people who had saved him would only speak of him with kind words.

* * *

$$Chapter\ 17$$

Raiqa was the only one who reached Rawalpindi. Out of her whole family, she was the only one who had survived. She had crossed over into Pakistan, and had arrived in Lahore. From there, she had taken a train to Rawalpindi. She and Rani had parted once they got off the train.

"Where will you go?" Raiqa had asked.

She smiled. "I will find someplace. I'll find somewhere to work where I can stay at their home."

But Raiqa was still worried. "Come to my sister's house until you find a place."

But she shook her head. "It's okay."

Her tone was firm. She was leaving no space to argue. "Then…" Raiqa looked around, spotting a ticket counter close by. "Wait here."

She hurried to the counter and asked for a piece of paper and a pen. She took them from the attendant and wrote down Najma's address. She had been to Hassan's house a little before Najma's marriage and had memorised the address of the house when she was there. "This is my sister's address," she told Rani, giving her the piece of paper. "If you need anything, come."

Rani took the paper. "Thank you. I'll get going now. You should too."

* * *

It was Najma who opened the door. She yelled out in relief when she first saw her. But then she saw her bloodied clothes and halted abruptly. She looked behind Raiqa for their family. "Ya Allah!" Aapa fell to the ground as the realisation hit.

Hassan Bhai quickly rushed to her side and supported her.

Raiqa stood there barely moving. "It's not their blood." She told her quickly. "I didn't see them die. But I saw many more."

"If you didn't see them die, then…" Hassan Bhai began.

"Don't you know how they are? They don't stab once… they aren't trying to scare us; they're out to kill. There isn't even anyone to come back for them to be rescued even if someone didn't die immediately. I heard on the train; there's no Muslim left in that neighbourhood."

Raiqa knew they had more questions but no strength to ask them. She saw Hassan Bhai wipe a tear away from his face, and then help Aapa up. No one spoke a word as Raiqa followed them both inside.

Aamna, Najma's mother-in-law and Asghar had been sitting inside and they had rushed out when they heard her voice. Raiqa saw Asghar's eyes shift from her to her sister and then to his brother as he tried to understand the situation.

She had kept going for so long, putting one foot in front of another. Now she was safe, in Najma's house, she dropped to the ground and sobbed. Great big sobs. Najma, Hassan and her family watched as her whole body shook. Najma dropped beside her.

"Amma?" asked Najma. Raiqa shook her head. "Abba?" Raiqa shook her head again.

"Daadi? Jamil?" Again Raiqa shook her head.

No one in Hassan's family asked Raiqa about what happened that had resulted in this loss. She was thankful for that. She knew, as they all sat there in silence, that they were grieving too. The relationship between the two families wasn't only one of in-laws; they had lived in the same neighbourhood for several years.

The neighbourhood.

Raiqa's mind kept repeating the last view she saw of the place she grew up. The dead bodies, the ones that had nobody to treat them with the normal respect.

Her family. All of them who tried until their last breath to protect one another. How could they all suddenly be gone?

Amma and Abba still had to marry her off. They had wanted to see Najma's kids, her kids, Jamil's kids...how could they not? Jamil, who had yet to grow up and fulfil his dreams of becoming an engineer. And Daadi, she said she was going to live a hundred years, whether they liked it or not. She still had so many years to go…How could she not be here?

That night, as she sat on the prayer mat, Raiqa cursed someone for the first time in her life. She cursed the ones who had killed her family, her friends, her innocent Muslim brothers and sisters. Like the one who killed that pregnant woman in front of her own eyes; Raiqa cursed them all.

* * *

It had been several days now. Raiqa knew that more and more people had been killed, not just Muslims in India, but Sikhs and Hindus were massacred too. She avoided hearing any news that Asghar or Hassan brought home. She had mostly kept herself locked in the small room that they had given her. Nobody forced her to come out or even bothered her. Najma was still grieving, so they barely saw each other despite living in the same house.

Raiqa couldn't sleep. She barely did these days. Every time she closed her eyes, she would see the same scene; the bloodied streets, the dead bodies. Sometimes, she would see the bodies of her family as well. It would be dark, and she would be walking and bump into something. When she looked down, she would see one of them. And then they would be all around her. Some people she knew, some she didn't. Just endless, vacant faces and dead bodies.

She didn't know what was worse, staying awake or falling asleep. Whatever she did, it felt like hell. She cried; she cried a lot at first. But whatever she did, the guilt didn't leave. The guilt of being the only one who survived. They had died; she should have too.

Najma's mother-in-law would come in three times a day, with breakfast, lunch and dinner. At first, she would just put the tray down and leave. After a few days, she realised that Raiqa didn't eat if she left right away. So now, she came in and sat next to her on the *charpai* and fed her one bite at a time. Neither of them spoke about it. She would leave the room as soon as Raiqa was finished.

After a couple of weeks, as she was leaving the room Raiqa said, "Thank you, Aamna Khala."

Aamna came back into the room, put her hand on Raiqa's knee, "Raiqa we grieve together. When you want to talk I am here. If you want someone to just sit with you, I am here."

Aamna continued to bring food to Raiqa and Raiqa would continue to say "Thank you, Aamna Khala," but that was all.

★ ★ ★

A few weeks later, Raiqa realised that even though she was safe, a lot of others weren't. The Muslims in Pakistan were ready to avenge the lives of their brothers and sisters who were slaughtered by attacking innocent Hindu and Sikh families on this side of the border.

"They aren't going to stop." Hassan and Asghar were both discussing the news one evening. "Three more Hindus were killed last night."

They had lived in a neighbourhood which was mainly Hindu. Only four of the houses were occupied by Muslim families, and the rest of the neighbourhood consisted mostly of Hindu and Sikh families. Since Hassan and his family had spent several years there, they were close to a lot of them. Raiqa understood why he was so worried about them. Losing a neighbour who was as close as family was extremely difficult. She was reminded again of all those she had lost…

Nasir Chacha… who was like another father to her. His family, Alia and her brothers whom she had played with back when she was a kid.

Suraiyya Khala… Haidar.

That night, she was awoken by a noise outside. It was the same howl she had heard back home. The howls that had meant death was coming. She quickly rushed out of her room and downstairs where everyone else had already gathered.

Najma Aapi began to weep as she cradled her bump. As Hassan Bhai ushered the women upstairs to be safe, she had a sense of déjà vu. Was this really happening again?

Would she survive this time?

It became pretty clear after a while that the attackers weren't there for them. They were locals who knew who lived in which houses because they only broke into the homes of the Hindu families. She closed her eyes and hugged her sister who whimpered at every scream. And there were many.

It was almost morning by the time the streets had gone silent. Everybody came down again, but no one said a word. It felt as if there was a pressure around her heart and it was becoming more and more difficult to breathe.

Hassan Bhai sat there, his face having become red from crying. Those people had come after his friends, and he hadn't been able to do anything about it.

Suddenly, there were screams outside again. "No! No, don't take me. My family is still in there. Ma! Abba!"

Raiqa didn't recognize the voice but everyone else did. Aamna's hand went up to her chest as she stared at their own closed door.

"Let me go!" the girl yelled again. "Let me go, you bastard!" Maybe the girl was someone precious to Aamna. She looked as if she was in pain, as if the girl outside was her own daughter.

Hassan Bhai and Asghar looked the same too.

The screams continued. "Aamna! Are you in there? Aamna save me! Aamna!"

Unable to hold herself anymore, Aamna got up and ran to the door but Najma was faster. She stood in front of her, blocking the door. "Don't open it, Aamna."

"Anjali!...They're taking her..."

Najma was shaking her head. "They have weapons, Aamna. If anyone of us tries to stop them, they won't hesitate in killing us. They have killed so many others already. They won't spare us."

"Aamna!" Anjali was still calling, her last desperate attempt to get help.

"Think about your own children, Aamna. Think about us. They'll kill us all."

"But what will they do to Anjali…"

"She'll get out. Allah will help her. Pray for her, Aamna. *Inshallah* she will get to the other side safely."

The screams eventually faded away. Aamna had fallen back to sitting on her *charpai*.. Najma collapsed right in front of the door and pulled her legs closer to her, sobbing. It wasn't long before Najma was wailing.

Nobody moved. Nobody tried to pick her up. Nobody tried to console anyone, they all just sat there. For a long time.

Raiqa looked at Najma and thought about her soon to be born child. Maybe it was him who she was trying to protect as well.

Time passed. August came and Pakistan emerged on the map as an independent state. Today they had sat together and listened to the first transmission of *Radio Pakistan*. Aapa and Aamna had broken down crying. None of them knew if they were crying happy tears or sad ones in memory of their loved ones. They just held each other and cried.

She couldn't help but think of Haidar as she touched the watch on her wrist again and again wondering if he had heard the radio too. "Happy Independence Day," she said under her breath.

Najma gave birth to a baby boy at the start of September. They named him Noman, a name Amma was particularly fond. She had always wanted to name Jamil, Noman but Abba had won that battle. Noman was the one ray of sunshine in Raiqa's life during this time. She would console herself by rocking Noman and talking softly to him. It was hard to stay miserable when Noman smiled up at her. However, she feared for Noman in a way she had never feared for anyone before.

Chapter 18

Hassan Bhai looked at Aamna, whose eyes had become so weary and full of sadness, and decided that he had lost too many people. They had been living in this house, this neighbourhood for several years now, but now the neighbourhood held too many memories, memories he would rather forget.

They had to move.

It was the next evening that Hassan Bhai and Asghar discussed where they should move. After much deliberation, it was decided that Karachi would be a good option. Now that where they would be going was settled, the conversation turned to business. Asghar was an engineer and had been able to put away a little money. He proposed setting up a business. Hassan offered to contribute financially to the business if he could be his partner. Only when everything had been decided did they tell Aamna, Najma and Raiqa about the plans. He made a point to make sure that Raiqa knew that she would be going as part of the family.

Hassan Bhai suggested that Asghar go and have a look. So, Asghar left for Karachi, and stayed with some family there. After a month, when he returned Raiqa was surprised by the amount of relief she felt that he had returned safely. Hassan Bhai and Aamna were happy to hear about how the family there were doing. He had found somewhere to live, a place to run the business from and had started to make business connections.

Najma, Aamna and Raiqa started packing up the house and plans were quickly made for the move.

Aamna found it difficult to pack up the house; emotionally she was a wreck. Sometimes, Hassan Bhai wondered if he was doing the right thing. She had been through so much already. However, she assured him that she needed the new start as much as he did, however difficult it was going to be.

* * *

When they reached Karachi, they were welcomed by family there. They quickly felt at home and a part of the community. It was December now, and there was still no news of Haidar. Time after time, someone would try to bring up the idea that Haidar, like so many others, hadn't made it, but Raiqa never let them finish.

"I have already lost my family," she would say. "Allah won't take him away from me too. I don't deserve that."

The people around her gave her pitying looks after she would say those words. She knew what the looks meant. They probably thought she was going crazy in her belief. She didn't say anything more than that though. It was best if she didn't say anything. Almost everyone around her had lost someone, family, or friends.

She could feel Haidar's presence. There was a part of her that knew he was still out there, somewhere, alive. She wondered where he was and what had happened to him. Every time she prayed, her *duas* was longer than her *namaz*. She would sit on the prayer mat for hours and pray for his safety. She hoped that he had somehow made it to Pakistan, even if he wasn't with her. She knew that even if he had reached Pakistan, there was no way for him to know that Najma's family was no longer in Rawalpindi. He had no way to know where she was.

He had no way of knowing if she was even alive.

He appeared in her dreams too... not exactly dreams. They were more like memories that played out in her head. Memories of the two of them on the roof. She wore the watch that he had given her all the time; it was heavy on her wrist and loose but her arm felt naked without it now. Just like the *taweez* that her mother had given her and her engagement ring, it was a part of her. She didn't care about all the questions that might be asked when she wore these items in front of the new neighbours.

Raiqa thought she should get a job. Although Hassan Bhai said that she wasn't a burden at all, she felt like she was. She knew she wasn't qualified for most traditional jobs, but she started tutoring a few kids under the age of twelve in the house's courtyard.

It kept her busy; it kept her mind off all the horrible things that had happened and the people she missed; and she earned enough to pay for her needs.

Noman was already three months old. The older he got the more his facial features began to resemble his maternal family. Aamna said that his eyes were exactly like Raiqa's, eyes that she had inherited from her father. Often, while Raiqa played with her nephew, she would notice that his laugh was like Jamil's and Abba's and that would taint her smile with a bit of sadness. If they were here, Abba would hold him on his shoulder, Amma would put kohl in his eyes and make him clothes and Jamil would play with him all day and night. But they weren't there. As more time passed, Najma began to think about Raiqa's marriage. She wasn't going to bring it up to Raiqa; she would wait until they asked her, which she knew would take a while.

Najma really hoped Haidar would show up by then. It was February by the time they first brought it up.

"I won't marry anyone but Haidar," Raiqa replied, making sure that she conveyed what she meant clearly.

Najma looked unhappily at her. Pity, she recognised the look by now. She realised that she hated pity.

Raiqa didn't sleep that night. She prayed with all her heart because that was the only thing she could do.

Najma left her alone after that. She decided to wait, hoping that Raiqa would come to terms with Haidar's 'death'.

* * *

The children she taught came around at four o clock. There weren't many of them, and all of them were under grade five so it was not a hard job. She needed something to do during the long early hours of the day and wondered if she could volunteer at the refugee camps. She made a mental note to ask Asghar or Hassan. The kids she taught did make her feel better though. Maybe it was because they didn't give her that one special look that the elders who knew what had happened gave her. The children would joke with her, would whine when she gave them homework or tests, would ask for pakoras sometimes and they would tell her stories of their schools. They treated her the same as they would have treated anyone her age.

Rabia Aapa, one of Najma's friends was a teacher at a nearby school, and her husband worked with Hassan Bhai. She and Najma would visit each other frequently. Although she knew a few other people in the neighbourhood, this was the only true friend Najma had in Karachi.

Raiqa didn't know a lot of people that they knew. When people came over, she would simply greet them and then go into her room. She didn't understand why she did this. She had always liked to meet new people but now, she didn't. There was an air of discomfort when she was around people she didn't know.

That night, as she and Najma sat together. Najma looked hesitant.

"Is something wrong?" Raiqa asked.

"Rabia Aapa asked for your hand for her brother." Najma broke the news quickly to her.

Raiqa paused in the process of bringing her hand up to her mouth to eat her roti. "What?"

Najma looked down, visibly uncomfortable. She had expected this reaction.

"Rabia Aapa, my friend who's the teacher…"

"I know who she is." Raiqa slid her plate to the side; she had suddenly lost her appetite. "Why would she ask that? And even if she did, why are you bringing this up to me?"

Aapa sighed, pulling up a chair to sit in front of her,. "I want you to consider it."

"I won't," she was adamant. "Are you that tired of me staying here?" She understood where her sister's heart came from; it wasn't that her intentions had an evil motive behind it. She knew how hard their parents' death had been on her too. Najma was only trying to be the parental figure in Raiqa's life now that their parents were gone. But she would rather Najma stayed her sister instead of trying to become her mother.

"No, it's not that. Of course not."

"I'll move somewhere else if you want me to."

She was mad, exasperated with it all. It hadn't even been a year since their parents had passed away. How could Najma bring up marriage? Especially when they didn't even know if Haidar was really…

"Don't be ridiculous, Raiqa." Aapa reached for her hand. "I will tell her no if you want me to. I will. I just…He didn't seem like a bad option, so I asked. I only want what's best for you."

Raiqa let out a sigh. "I don't know what's best for me, Aapa. I feel useless as it is. But getting married to someone… I can't. I know what you all believe about Haidar being…" She couldn't even say it. "Anyway, my heart can't accept it. I feel like he'll be here. Someday. Maybe not as soon as I would like, but he'll be here."

Raiqa saw Najma shed a tear before she got up and turned away. Raiqa looked back to her food. Realising she wasn't hungry anymore, she quietly got up and left the kitchen and quickly headed up to her room.

She stared at the watch, the only object she owned that belonged to Haidar. The letters that he had sent were still back at her parents' home. And if she hadn't been wearing his watch that day, it wouldn't be with her now. The ring she wore had a special meaning too, but it had never belonged to him. He had worn the watch. It had once been on his own wrist. The leather of the watch had touched him, the metal dial had been against his skin. Every time she saw it, she would remember the promise he made to her. His promise that he would marry her when he got back.

And he would.

Chapter 19

It was the evening of 27th of April, 1948. Palvindar had gone to Kanganpur. The children were playing in a corner and Ma Ji had already gone to bed after working on the farm all day. Haidar planned to go to bed too. He was only waiting to pray his Isha prayer.

Palvindar reached home around eight, looking oddly excited about something. Now that Haidar had come to know him, he had realised that his host was an easy-going man whose smile came easily. But even in his nine-month stay here, he hadn't seen him look this animated.

"Did you get a good price?"

Palvindar came to sit next to him. "I got something better."

He laughed at how happy the person in front of him looked. "What?"

He reached into his pocket and pulled out a piece of paper, handing it to Haidar. It was a train ticket.

"You can go home now."

Haidar stared at the ticket in his hand, the train ticket to Rawalpindi, and then back at Palvindar, who was beaming. "The situation is better now. I should have sent you earlier but...the crop..."

At the start of the year, Palvindar had suffered a major financial loss when his crop went bad. It had become a hard time for the family. But Palvindar's strong will had helped him to start over.

"Thank you," Stunned, it was all Haidar could say.

He already knew why Palvindar hadn't sent him at the start of the year. He was in a bad situation himself so Haidar hadn't even thought about leaving then. He didn't know how much help he had been to him, but he was glad that he could do something. He knew that he wouldn't ever be able to repay Palvindar for all his help and care, but he wasn't selfish to leave him at a time like that.

"You should head for the city tomorrow. The train departs tomorrow night."

He nodded as Palvindar reached forward to hug him. "Thank you, brother."

He wanted to thank him more. He hadn't done anything for him really. It was Palvindar who had protected him, had given him shelter.

That night, along with his regular namaz, he prayed an additional two nafl of thanks. He stayed on the praying mat for hours, thanking God for saving him, for giving him a friend like Palvindar. "Keep them safe," he prayed. "Keep them happy." Palvindar dropped him off at the train station. Haidar's last goodbyes to everyone else left him with a feeling of sadness. Even though none of them mentioned it, they all knew that this was the last time that they would ever see each other. They would just be memories. Memories that would be hard to reminisce because they were connected to the biggest tragedy of their lives.

"Take care of yourself, Putr." Ma Ji patted his shoulders and looked up at him through her sad, old eyes. "Go home and even if it's hard there at first, don't forget to take care of yourself. Your God, whom you prayed to so much, will make things turn out well. Raiqa will be healthy and alive."

His heart skipped a beat as Ma Ji mentioned Raiqa. It had almost been a year since he had heard anything about her. It hadn't been easy.

He thought about her all the time, wondering how she was. He never let his mind wander to other possibilities other than her being safe and sound at Najma's place.

The little ones had helped their grandmother prepare food for him to eat on his way. Yuvraj brought it to him. "Eat it well, Bhaiya."

He stroked their heads. His affection for the children had grown as well. They were well-behaved, considerate and mature for their age. He hoped that they would grow up well. They had already lost their mother, another tragedy would break them. Palvindar hugged Haidar goodbye at the station one last time before he boarded the train. He remained there on the platform until the train started to move. The last thing Haidar saw was his friend waving at him with a huge smile on his face. "Thank you." Haidar whispered even though Palvindar couldn't hear him.

* * *

He said a prayer of thanks as soon as he set foot on the ground. He wasn't in danger anymore; he was in Pakistan. Somehow it already felt like home. The station wasn't crowded; nobody was waiting for those who were arriving. The travellers only hoped that their loved ones stuck in India would somehow manage to come to Pakistan where they would be together again. He knew that right now everyone who was getting off the train was relieved. Relieved that they had made it. It didn't matter if they had sat on the train's floor or not, what mattered was that they had reached a place that was safe.

Haidar glanced at his reflection in the glass door. He no longer looked like what he used to. Although he had shaved and cut his hair, the scars on his body were reminders that the times weren't as they used to be. And though he was relieved, he couldn't allow himself to be happy. How could he be, when he was still all alone?

Raiqa.

Her name that had kept him going. She was alive; she had to be.

There was no way he could be sure. He could only hope, only pray. He hadn't seen her dead body, which meant that she had escaped from the house. He only hoped that she had escaped the city. Every time he thought of the stories that Palvindar's neighbours brought in, he felt a shiver run down his body.

She was safe, he kept telling himself. She was okay.

Now in Rawalpindi, he had no idea where to go. He had been to the house before to visit Asghar, but Asghar had always met him at the station and that was before Pakistan had been created. The area had changed so much. The thought hadn't occurred to him before. He looked around but nothing looked familiar. He believed things would be easy once he got to Pakistan but reality him; he had no idea where she would be. Pakistan was a whole country.

Without knowing where he was heading, he left the train station. He had to find a place to stay. He didn't have much with him, just a small trunk with a few clothes that Palvindar had bought him. Other than that, he had nothing.

Outside he heard the *muazzen* start the *Azaan*, the call to prayer.

It had been a while since he heard it. He had been guessing at the correct times to pray when he was at Palvindar's house. The timings of the prayers changed as winter approached so he could only speculate. He tried to pray as early and as long as possible so he wouldn't be praying at the wrong time.

His feet began to move towards the mosque of their own accord. He could see the minaret from a distance and knew that, at least for now, that was where he was going.

He prayed in congregation for the first time in months. He felt safe. He was surrounded by his own people. Even back at Palvindar's. he could never bring himself to be too at home. He came to trust the family he was staying with, yes, but he was worried about the other people in the village who knew he was staying there attacking him. Sometimes, he couldn't even sleep. He thought of how his family had probably been sleeping when they were attacked. Not just them, the whole neighbourhood.

He stayed in the mosque long after he had finished praying. He didn't have a home here, but right now he felt at home.

* * *

They had left.

Asghar's family no longer lived where they used to. He had managed to get there with only a little difficulty. Luckily when he had been asking around, he found someone who knew Hassan and where he lived. After he reached their road it didn't take long for him to spot the house.

The gate, however held a big lock.

He had to ask vendors and shopkeepers nearby if anybody knew where they had gone. There were only a few people left in the neighbourhood who had known them, but nobody knew where exactly they had gone. Some remembered Hassan mentioning Peshawar, but then another would argue and say it was Hyderabad.

Haidar walked back to the mosque with a heavy heart. They had left. And he wasn't sure where they were.

Days passed. Haidar tried not to think a lot about it. Instead, he focused on finding a job and a place to live. He soon started to teach at a small school. The pay wasn't much but it was better than nothing. Although he had to share with three other guys, he had somewhere to live and it had a roof.

The hope still remained that one day he would find out where she was and run to her. He prayed for a miracle every night.

He missed her more than ever. He was afraid that she would fade from his memory. That one day he would only have a vague idea of what she looked like. He reminded himself of her beautiful eyes, her long hair, her smile. Every single thing about her that he loved.

I'll make it. I've made it this far. I'll make it to her.

* * *

Chapter 20

Sometimes, it felt as if Asghar was the only one who understood the situation she was in. Raiqa knew that there was a part of him who still believed that his friend was alive as well. They didn't get into long conversations often, but when they did, they would talk about Haidar. Unlike the others, he didn't talk about him in past tense.

She respected Asghar. He didn't mention it much, but she knew that he had lost a lot of friends. Sometimes she wondered if he had lost someone really important to him too. He wasn't engaged, but was he in love with someone that was no longer there?

He had become quieter ever since she had arrived in Rawalpindi. She had always remembered him as someone who was easy going with a ready smile, but these days, it felt like he barely did. He was almost always working. It was times like these that Raiqa wished she could drown herself in work too. Maybe then, she wouldn't be such a mess.

That night, Raiqa and Asghar sat in the living room. Hassan wasn't home yet; Aamna had already gone to sleep; and Najma was putting Noman to bed.

"Asghar?" She asked.

"Hm?"

"What do you think we would have been doing if we were all here? If we had all made it to Pakistan."

His lips went up in a small smile. "I think it would be about time for me to get married now," he joked. "Don't you think?"

"You can still get married. Do you want us to look for a girl?"

His smile turned sad. "Let's not."

"Did you…have someone you…"

He nodded. "Maybe Aamna hasn't mentioned it in front of anyone but there was this girl. Back when we were kids, our parents were hoping that we would marry when we grew up. I would have wanted to… all the time I spent with her was the best time of my life. We would have become engaged very soon if nothing had happened…"

"Did she…" She trailed off without finishing the question, but he understood.

"That's the thing. I don't know. I don't know if she made it or not. I don't know if she's still in India or if she made it to Pakistan. Every time I get a letter, I wonder if it's from her. Then it hits me that she doesn't even know where I am."

Both of us are in the same boat, she thought. Maybe that's why they could sit together and have this conversation. They could empathise with each other but knew not to sympathise.

"When I think of Haidar, it's the same. He doesn't know where we are, and we don't know where he is. It's frustrating, isn't it?"

"Very frustrating."

"But there's this hope, you know. I don't know what I would be like if somehow I find out that he's…"

"Yeah… me either. You know, back when we were studying, we would make so many plans together. Like, we didn't even have to think twice before saying 'when I turn fifty, I'll…' He used to say that once we got married our wives would end up being friends as well. He always talked about introducing you to me, and I had to remind him that I already knew you. I think he was a little jealous of the fact that I had known you before he did. And now, I am here and you're here and… well, the situation isn't what we had imagined at all."

"He told me he wanted to introduce us too." She laughed. "I reminded him just like you did."

"After you two got engaged, he would talk about you a lot. We teased him of course, but I was so happy for him. Us friends, we had this whole thing planned out. We were going to embarrass him at your wedding."

Raiqa had imagined her wedding too, many times. She would imagine herself in a red dress and him in a *shervani*. She had imagined saying 'I do' in front of the mullah. She had imagined her father and brother sending her away under the Quran. And everything else a girl about to get married would do, she imagined that too.

But the day had never come.

"Asghar?"

"Hm?"

"Do you think that he's still alive?"

He looked at her with a sad smile. "I don't know, *Bhabi*. I really don't."

He had called her *Bhabi* – sister-in-law – for the first time. Maybe at that moment, he was missing his friend the same way she was missing him. Maybe right now, he wasn't looking at her as someone he had played with when they were kids. He was looking at her as if he was searching for his own friend. Like she was a reminder of Haidar.

That night, he appeared in her dreams. He told her that they were going to get married, that he had already arranged the Mullah.

"No more tears from now on, okay? Everything is going to be okay," Haidar whispered to her.

But then it grew dark and the hand that had taken hers disappeared. She was left alone. Again.

★ ★ ★

Chapter 21

Haidar was exhausted when he came back from school that day. All his life, he had enjoyed spending time with children. That was until he started teaching them. Every day he would realise that teaching wasn't for him at all. He would easily get irritated when having to explain something more than twice. But he tried to keep his frustration to himself.

That day, he barely had time to take a shower after coming back. Apart from one of his roommates, who was currently jobless, the rest were usually at work when he came back so the room was usually silent. He took a quick shower and then went out to pray.

After Zuhr, he was starving, and he decided to get something from a nearby stand.

"Arif Bhai, a plate please. 2 rotis."

The familiar man nodded and went to work preparing his food. The man owned a small stand, but the food was cheap and it was all Haidar could afford at the moment. He was already paying so much rent for his small room, and the school job didn't pay much. He only knew how to cook *daal* which was what he ate most days. He would usually just stop at the stand for breakfast, sitting for a few minutes for chai before he went to work. When he didn't have time to cook, he would come to Arif Bhai's at the corner of the street.

He could smell the *aloo gosht* before the food reached him and his stomach rumbled. There were always two dishes at the stand; one of them would be a rice dish and the other would be a vegetable dish.

"Two rotis please," he heard another voice call out. Without meaning to, he looked at the new arrival. He couldn't believe who he saw.

"Asghar." The name left his mouth, barely audible even to himself. It was him. His hair was shorter than he remembered it and he had grown a small stubble, but it was definitely him. It was his friend.

Asghar looked around after he was done ordering, looking for a seat. There weren't many places to sit anyway. Just two tables and a few chairs. It didn't take him long to spot Haidar.

He froze. Haidar saw his lips form his name.

He stood up slowly, a smile making way to his face at the reunion with one of his closest friends.

It was about time.

* * *

"We moved a few months ago. I guess… I guess Bhai wanted to start afresh. He lost a lot people… It was hard for all of us. We even thought you…"

He didn't continue, looking down instead. Haidar knew how he felt. To not know if someone was alive or not, and then comes a time when the only logical thought ends up being acceptance.

"Is…Is Raiqa…?" He was afraid to ask.

"She's alive. She's fine."

Haidar felt the biggest wave of relief that he had ever felt. His biggest fear had been reaching Pakistan and finding out that Raiqa had never made it. The thought of it had given him nightmares.

"She refused to believe that you were dead." Asghar laughed. "She said that her heart said you were alive. There were some proposals, though." He looked up at him hesitantly.

Haidar didn't meet his eye. He couldn't just pretend that this didn't faze him at all. "And?"

"And just that. Bhabi didn't want to force her into anything. And Raiqa wasn't willing to listen."

"I heard that her family…"

"They didn't make it."

Even though he had known that, hearing it from Asghar as confirmation hurt more. A dark shadow crossed Asghar's face as well. "Did they send Raiqa early?"

Asghar shook his head. "When they were attacked, Rasheeda Khala and Daadi told her to jump to the next house, Nasir Chacha's roof. She hid there for some time and managed to survive. Maybe it was luck… she went through a lot."

There was silence. Haidar's heart hurt. He couldn't imagine having to be there while your family was murdered and not being able to do anything about it. "How is she now?"

"She's…" Asghar paused, thinking. "It feels like she grew up suddenly. She's quiet. But she's better than she was when we came here. What about you?"

The food that was now in front of them had remained untouched. "I went back. To Firozpur ."

"Your parents…"

He looked down, remembering their bloody bodies, how it looked like they had died trying to protect each other. A scene that had haunted him in his nightmares. "I saw them." He gulped. There was a pause. "Then I was taking a train to Rawalpindi. It was attacked. I got hurt and passed out. A Sikh family from a nearby village took me in. They took care of me."

"Thank God you were found by the right people, then. If you hadn't been rescued…"

"I would have died. If not of the wounds, maybe of hunger."

He was aware that if Palvindar's family hadn't found him, he wouldn't be sitting there.

"Why did it take so long for you to come?"

"A lot happened…"

"Well, we don't need to think about any of that. You're here now, and that's all that matters."

He smiled. He kept looking at Asghar every few seconds. A part of him still found it hard to the believe that he was really there.

"Do you have a job?"

"Not a very good one. I teach." Asghar smiled. He looked amused. "What?"

"Raiqa teaches too. She teaches the children in the neighbourhood."

He couldn't help but smile at that. She was probably better with children than he was. But then he thought of how Raiqa and Jamil were together. Bickering and teasing all day long, something he had never experienced himself. Maybe she was just as bad with children as he was.

"You'll come to Karachi with me, right?" Asghar looked hopeful. He wasn't expecting a negative answer.

"I have to meet her but can I just... move there?"

Although he was not living very well now, it would be harder for him to move to a new city alone.

"Hassan Bhai and I recently started a business. It's a small one, but we would love it if you could lend a hand."

"I don't know anything about business."

"You probably know more than I do. You were more interested in it even while you were studying engineering, weren't you?"

"But..."

"There's not a lot of us left. There are so many people that I'm not even sure if they're alive or not. Come with me, please." Haidar wanted to. He wasn't even sure why he was hesitating.

Asghar's family were the only people he knew from home. She was in Karachi too.

"You can find a house close to ours… or even if you don't… just somewhere in the city. Hassan Bhai will be glad to have you in the business. Everybody needs family."

He knew that. He needed family.

* * *

Chapter 22

Nobody else was home. Najma and her mother-in-law had been invited to a wedding. Aamna felt isolated not knowing very many people in their new neighbourhood, so when the family who lived next door invited them to their son's wedding, she was overjoyed. Hassan Bhai was still not back from work; he had been working late this week and Asghar was still to return from Rawalpindi.

Raiqa went into the kitchen only to come out soon after when she realised that there was nothing to eat. Not knowing what else to do, she decided to listen to the radio.

She was almost asleep when she heard the door open. The sound was followed by footsteps. It sounded like there were at least two newcomers in the house, but the footsteps were too heavy to be Najma's and Aamna's.

She saw Asghar before she saw him. He was trailing behind like he was scared to come in.

He looked different. She didn't remember a scar on the left side of his face, neither did she remember his stubble. His face looked aged, there was a certain maturity to it that she didn't recognize from a year ago.

But it was him. Haidar. Her Haidar.

Out of the corner of her eye, she noticed Asghar leave, maybe to give them privacy.

She didn't remember standing up but suddenly she was on her feet and right in front him.

He was there.

She saw a tear leave his eye and realised that a few had fallen from her own too. She lifted her hand to touch his face, expecting him to disappear. It felt like a dream. A dream too good to be true. A dream that she didn't want to wake up from.

But he was there.

Her hand touched his face. His beautiful face. She wiped the tear that had fallen and then the scar that wasn't there before. She didn't blink, in fear that he would disappear.

"You're here."

He smiled, a familiar sight that she had dearly missed. She wondered if she would wake up now. She didn't want to. She would rather die like this, with him than wake up.

"I missed you."

That did it. Those three words broke her. Suddenly, she was bawling.

He reached for her hand that was still touching his face and held it tightly. He kept looking at her, like he had been starved. She was doing the same, taking in the sight of his face like there was no tomorrow.

Only now there was, and it would be a good tomorrow. She would keep him close from now on so he wouldn't go away.

"I missed you so much," He repeated. He wrapped his arms around her and pulled her close, hugging her tightly. She held on to the fabric at the back of his shirt tightly, burying her head in his chest.

The hug felt familiar, even though they had never done it before. Their relationship had only needed their hearts. That was all they had ever needed. Each other. Knowing that their feelings were reciprocated; that they were each other's and each other's only.

It felt as though her body fit right into his arms like she was made for him. And he was made for her.

"I love you."

The words they had never directly said to each other, not on paper, not face to face. The words that she regretted never telling him. But she would do it now. She would say it over and over.

"I love you. I love you. I love you." The words came out muffled with her head in his chest, but he heard her.

And they stood there hugging and crying for a long time.

* * *

Aamna had broken down at the sight of Haidar. She had embraced him and kissed his head multiple times, thanking God over and over.

Najma and Aamna had returned around eleven at night. Raiqa and Haidar had been sitting outside. Aamna had mistaken his silhouette as Asghar's because it was dark but when he stood up, she gasped. She couldn't say anything for a while. She just stood there with her arms wide open.

Now, the entire family gathered in Aamna's bedroom. Raiqa noticed all of them turning their heads to look at Haidar again and again to make sure it was really him. She realised that she had been doing the same.

He was holding Aamna's hand and she was asking him how he had been, where he had gone, what he had been doing. Aamna could tell that he had missed being around familiar people.

He had been close to Asghar's family, Raiqa knew that. He used to visit them during holidays and would stay there for the weekend when they were in college. She had heard Aamna say that he was like her third son.

"Our Raiqa was right," Aamna was saying. "She knew you were alive."

Haidar looked at her and smiled. She stood at the corner of the room watching them and feeling an odd sense of fulfilment at the sight.

That night, she couldn't sleep. The small part of the fear that this all still might just turn out to be a dream kept her up. Next to her, Najma and Noman had already fallen asleep.

Hassan Bhai had let Haidar take his bed in the room he shared with Asghar and slept outside.

She ended up going outside to walk off some of her anxiety. As she quietly tiptoed out of her room, she saw Haidar leaving his.

"Can't sleep?" He mouthed. She nodded.

"Me neither."

She smiled and then gestured him to follow her. She led him up the stairs to a small open area. They always seemed to end up on rooftops.

He seemed to be thinking the same thing, and they laughed as their eyes met.

"You're still wearing it." He had noticed his watch on her wrist when she had lifted her hand to cover her face when she laughed.

"It's a part of me now," she told him honestly. "I feel empty without it."

"It was my promise," he reminisced, his eyes still on the watch. "I said I'd come to marry you. I wasn't able to keep it."

She shook her head. "You had said that when you came back, you would marry me," she reminded him. "You may be a little late. But you haven't broken your promise, yet."

They sat down on the ground. The night was bright, and she could see his lips go up in a small smile.

"When did you come to Rawalpindi?" She decided not to ask of his time before that. She didn't want them to start thinking about the tragedies they had been through.

"It's only been a short while. I taught at a school. I was planning to get a better job, though. I didn't spend that much time studying for all of it to go to waste." He sounded a little bitter.

"Teaching isn't that bad."

"Try teaching a class of forty."

She laughed. "You're here now. You can help Hassan Bhai instead. You always wanted to try your hand in business."

He nodded. "That's the plan."

"He could use all the help he can get. It's not easy setting up a business. He had some savings that he invested. You never know when you will need it, so it came in handy."

Haidar sighed. "Sometimes, even those savings can't help. When I was in Rawalpindi, it felt like I had left everything behind in India. I would have given all my savings to save them…"

Here they were. As much as Raiqa had wanted to avoid the topic, the truth was that they simply couldn't. There is no way to disregard a tragedy like that and move on like nothing had happened.

"You saw them?"

At first, she wasn't sure if he had heard her. There was silence as they both sat on the floor with their backs against the wall next to each other. It was after a while that he answered. "I did."

Raiqa didn't want to imagine what that would have been like. To reach home hoping with all your heart that the people you loved had lived. The sight of them dead would suck the life out of you; the hope of them being alive being shattered by a sight like that… it hurt to even think about it.

"They were holding each other," Haidar was saying, looking at the space ahead. "They would have begged for them to spare the other, I know they would. They were trying to protect each other." His voice cracked. He paused before he continued. "There was so much blood. How could somebody be so cruel to see all that blood and live with the fact that they spilled it? How does one live knowing that they killed so many people?"

Raiqa didn't say anything. She could feel the tears welling up. She had asked herself that question so many times.

"But again… it's not like I am completely clean." Her head turned to him quickly.

"I let Lubna Aapa die for me," he was saying. "I didn't even try to save her." He began to sob. "She died for me and I didn't even try to save her. I was too scared for my own life."

Raiqa closed her eyes, holding back a sob of her own. She had never known how Lubna had died. She had always assumed that she had been murdered with her family as well. That's what she had heard anyway. Their entire neighbourhood had been massacred.

"I hid… I hid like a coward."

She wiped a tear from her face and reached out to grab his hand. "It wasn't your fault."

"That doesn't mean I couldn't have done anything." He closed his eyes and hit the back of his head on the wall. "I should have done something."

She squeezed his hand. "I don't think she would have wanted you to. You said she was trying to save your life, right? She wouldn't have wanted you to put yourself in danger."

It hurt to watch him relive this. Raiqa had never seen him cry and she didn't want to ever again.

"You know I haven't cried for my parents yet? Not like I should have," he confessed.

Raiqa thought back to the nights she had spent crying. She wouldn't have been okay if she hadn't.

She pulled him close to her, resting his head on her shoulder and held him.

That night, he cried for them. She could tell as she stroked the back of his head how much he needed to. She knew he was crying for his parents, for her own, for Lubna Aapa and her family, for Nasir Chacha and Jamil too. He cried for everyone who didn't deserve to die but suffered because of the hatred some people had towards them.

And she cried with him.

* * *

Chapter 23

The night before their *Nikkah*, Raiqa had a dream about their parents. They were all there: Amma, Abba, Suraiyya Khala, Siddiqui Khalu and Jamil. They didn't say anything; a part of her wished they had. They all just smiled as if telling her that it would be alright from now on. That the bad times were over. From now on, there would only be good days.

This was the first time her parents had appeared in a good dream. Before that, she had only seen their faces in her nightmares, dead and lifeless.

She had breakfast with her sister that day. Asghar and Hassan Bhai were taking care of the arrangements, and Aamna had gone over the place that Haidar had bought. The place where Raiqa would be moving tonight.

"You good?" Najma asked.

"Amma and Abba were in my dream too. Suraiyya Khala, Siddiqui Khalu and Jamil too…"

"What did they say?"

"Nothing. They just seemed happy for me."

"They are. If they were here right now, Amma would be freaking out with the preparations. Suraiyya Khala would be over the moon, and you and Jamil would probably still be arguing."

She smiled, but her heart felt heavy. Suddenly she missed them more.

That night, Najma put the same jewellery on Raiqa as their mother had placed on her. Although the jewellery was ornate, Raiqa had dressed quite simply otherwise. A plain, white shalwar kameez with a red dupatta that had gold lace on the sides.

Raiqa and Haidar got married in late July, on the same day that they were supposed to get married a year earlier. Although the financial conditions weren't the best, they weren't too bad either. Aamna and Hassan Bhai both had savings, a portion of which they loaned to Haidar.

The wedding ceremony was simple, and there weren't many people. It was only the two families and a few other people from the neighbourhood. Those who did were filled with sadness at the memories of those who should have been there but weren't. Asghar and Bibi decided to come as the baraat while Najma Aapi and Hassan were the representatives of the bride's side.

Around seven, everybody had arrived and were already seated outside.

The mullah, she vaguely recognized, and the others entered the room she sat in around eight. Najma showed the mullah to a chair that sat next to the bed Raiqa was on. The rest of the men remained standing. Hassan gestured to the mullah to proceed with the *nikkah*.

She felt a pleasant nervousness as the mullah gave his blessings. There was a feeling of relief. Of happiness.

"Do you, Raiqa Kareem daughter of Zubeida Kareem, accept Haidar Malik, son of Siddiqui Malik as your husband?"

"I do."

The mullah repeated the question again. "I do."

And then the third time. "I do."

She signed her name on the wedding contract. Seeing her own name next to his brought her joy. She signed each letter carefully, for these were papers she had waited a year to sign. Najma was smiling widely at her the entire time. After the mullah left, she wrapped her arms around Raiqa. "*Mubarakbad,*" she congratulated her. "I wish you a lifetime of happiness."

"Thank you." Raiqa smiled, a new feeling of home settling in. She was now officially his wife. Haidar's wife.

They were married.

* * *

Aamna had helped Haidar decorate his room. Along with Asghar, she had spent days with Haidar picking out furniture and other necessities. They had mostly bought second-hand items, but Raiqa knew that Aamna wasn't the kind to settle for something defective. Aamna would have made sure that everything was in good enough condition to be used for the next five years at least.

Asghar and Aamna had accompanied Raiqa to her new home but had left soon after. Before they went, Aamna had told the new couple that she would send breakfast the next morning so they shouldn't worry about that.

Raiqa sat on the bed in her new bedroom, looking into the mirror and made sure that her dupatta was still properly pinned and the strands of hair falling to the side of her face were still in place. Haidar had gone to lock the door behind Aamna and Asghar.

He entered the room she was in a little while later, and Raiqa appreciated how good he looked. This was the first time they were alone all day.

Hassan had helped Haidar pick his *sherwani*, a plain black one. At this point, Raiqa was sure that he didn't wear the clothes but the clothes wore him. He was the kind of man that made bad attires look good.

He sat down in front of her. "Assalam o Alaikum," he greeted her with a big smile.

"Walaikum Salam," she replied. There was an almost tangible feeling in the air. It was hard to pinpoint what that feeling was. It was a mixture of love, sadness, joy and relief. She felt shy.

He reached for his pocket, pulling out a box. He brought out his hand, asking her to give him hers. She did.

He opened the box. There was a single *kangan* in there that he took out and carefully put on her wrist. "It's not gold, but I'll buy you one soon. I promise."

She shook her head. "It's okay. I like this one."

"You do?"

She nodded. "I do. I guess this will replace the watch I was wearing." She stroked it. "It reminds me of the one Amma used to wear."

He reached for her hand again, holding it gently in his own. "They would be really happy today, wouldn't they?"

"Hm," she said. "They are probably watching us from above right now. I like to think that they're all together, watching over us."

"I wouldn't be surprised if they were." He was looking right into her eyes. "That makes me want to be better. To make you the happiest girl. My mother once said that she would treat you like her own daughter. I know she would want me to take care of you on behalf of all of us."

"It won't be too difficult. I'm not that hard to please," she joked. Thinking of Suraiyya Khala she added, "I am going to take care of you on behalf of all of us too. I won't want her to be disappointed in me."

"I don't think that's possible," he assured her. "She loved you too much. She would have been the happiest today."

He was still holding her hand, stroking her knuckles absent- mindedly. She tightened her grip on his. "She would be happy. I hope she knows that after all of this, I won't let you get hurt again. I'll take care of you. And I'll make you happy."

He smiled. "You already do."

She looked deeply into his eyes. They were like windows to his heart, all she saw in them was love. His love for her. She lifted her hand and touched his face. "I love you."

This was the first time she had said it to him first. And she meant it with all her heart, with every single bone in her body. She loved him. She loved him to death.

And he was hers.

His eyes were gazing back into hers, and she knew he was thinking the same. He came closer, so close that their noses touched. "I love you too."

And at that moment, that was all that mattered.

★ ★ ★

Glossary

aapa Older sister.

aapa / baji Sister.

abba Father, dad.

adaab A polite, respectful greeting.

alhamdulillah An Arabic phrase meaning "praise be to God", sometimes translated as "thank God".

amma Mother, mum.

Asr The afternoon Islamic prayer.

Assalam o Alaikum I greet you.

Azaan The call to prayer.

bachay / bacha Kid. Informal for child.

bahu Daughter-in-law.

besharam Shameless.

beta Son.

beti Daughter

bhabi Sister-in-law

bhai Brother.

bhaiya Brother.

chador   A large piece of cloth that is wrapped around the head and upper body leaving only the face exposed.

charpai   Bed, usually wooden.

daadi   Grandmother

Devutthana Ekadashi   A Hindu fast and celebration.

dupatta   A shawl, commonly worn as part of a salwar kameez.

eidi   A gift given to children during Eid.

haleem   A type of meat stew.

haveli   A home.

haya   Humility

Isha   Night prayer

jan   Life

jinn   A type of spirit

kaju   Cashew nuts

kangan   Bracelet

kenari   Edge

khala   Aunt

khalu   Uncle

khoobsoorat   Gorgeous

Khuda Hafiz   God protect you

kurta   Male clothing similar to the Shalwar Kameez.

lehenga   A full ankle-length skirt, usually worn on formal or ceremonial occasions

mithai   Sweets

mitr   Friend

muazzen   The official who proclaims the call to prayer mubarakbad   Congratulations

Mullah   A Muslim learned in Islamic theology; the head of a mosque

namaz   Prayer

putr   Son

roti   Bread, especially a flat round bread cooked on a griddle

sahib   A polite title for a man

salam   Peace

seviyan   Thin noodles.

shab bakhair   Goodnight

shalwar kameez   A long tunic worn over a pair of baggy trousers

sharmeeli   Shy

sherwani   A knee-length coat buttoning to the neck

sukriya   Thank you

sundar   Beautiful

tilaka   Hindu symbol placed on forehead

Walaikum Salam   Here you are healthy. Used as a greeting.

Zuhr   Midday prayer

www.ingramcontent.com/pod-product-compliance
Lightning Source LLC
Chambersburg PA
CBHW071922130726
47909CB00014B/2509